Praise for *The Source of Trouble.*

"Debra Monroe is a fierce writer. . . . She writes dialogue as if stitching samplers for our rawest truths, at once mean and exalted."
—Ron Carlson, author of
Plan B for the Middle Class

". . . terse but witty tales . . . one is diverted by these self-revealing characters who unfold their make-do philosophies of life."
—*Publishers Weekly*

"There's compassion, humor, and genuine amazement in the voices that speak these well-written stories. . . . Monroe's style is a highly readable blend of minimalism . . . and lyricism of a funny, down-to-earth kind."
—*Belles Lettres*

"Although she devotes most of her energy to creating the wry women whose half-funny, half-desperate voices dominate this book, Monroe's most appealing characters are probably the ardent, put-upon men who are devoted to those women. . . . the sympathy with which she writes about men endows these stories with a richness lacking in the work of many, if not most, of the writers who take as their subject the vagaries of the human heart."
—*Chicago Tribune*

"Strong stories full of lively characters."
—W. P. Kinsella, author of
Shoeless Joe

"Monroe seems to . . . build the backgrounds—the ramshackle apartment houses or the dusty fields of weeds behind a tavern—with a smattering of props and a few sensory nuances that set the scenes, all slightly shadowy, so that the characters . . . dominate. *The Source of Trouble* is an absorbing and memorable collection of stories . . ."
—*The Manhattan (Kansas) Mercury*

". . . stories invented by a mind as fecund and compellingly entertaining as her best characters."
—*Remark*

". . . ten stories that introduce a distinctive stylist whose bumpy-jumpy yet fluid prose tells of small-town and rural women who don't quite understand the trouble they're in as they hurry through relationships with men. . . . the resulting joys and heartaches are moving, not merely inevitable.

Monroe's voice, with its quirky leaps from the colloquial into poetry, can go the distance."
—*Kirkus Reviews*

"These stories are earthy without being mundane, full of wry humor and grim reality. . . . the reader gets the feeling that with Monroe's pen on their side, the protagonists can make it through any ordeal, their spirits as strong as the woman's voice creating them."
—*Charlotte Observer*

". . . this collection of ten stories is compelling and powerful."
—*University Press Book News*

"Monroe's brilliance shines in her conversational style, as if she's telling you the story over a cool beer, rocking on the front porch on a hot August day. Her descriptive passages cry to be heard."
—*Salt Lake City Tribune*

Also by Debra Monroe

A Wild, Cold State

The Source of Trouble

Debra Monroe

Scribner Paperback Fiction
Published by Simon & Schuster
New York   London   Toronto   Sydney   Tokyo   Singapore

SCRIBNER PAPERBACK FICTION
Simon & Schuster Inc.
Rockefeller Center
1230 Avenue of the Americas
New York, NY 10020

First Scribner Paperback Fiction Edition 1995

SCRIBNER PAPERBACK FICTION and design is a registered trademark of Simon & Schuster Inc.

Manufactured in the United States of America

10   9   8   7   6   5   4   3   2   1

ISBN 0-671-89716-0

Some of these stories first appeared in the following magazines: "Trouble" in the *Santa Monica Review;* "The Source of Trouble" in *Great Stream Review,* "This Far North" in *St. Andrew's Review;* "Starbuck" in the *North Dakota Quarterly;* and "Enough" in *Touchstone.* The poem "Tattoo," in the story "A Pious Wish," was originally published in the *Apalachee Quarterly.*

Contents

The Source of Trouble

My Sister Had Seven Husbands

Number One, Lance.

But first let me make this clear: it's more than a headline in a bright-colored tabloid, BABY FOUND IN WOMB WITH WOODEN LEG. Or a blurb on the third page of a quality newspaper: WOMAN WEDS FOR 34TH TIME (I'm in Love with Love, says Blushing Bride). It was seven times, something any of us might do if our lives were higgledy-piggledy enough, like Amelia's, or if God had given us what he gave her, a soul too nerveless to stand the sight of much: anything frail or newborn; blood spilled, real or imagined; men committing adultery, our father, for instance, my own husband Ralph. It was like keeping up with Liz Taylor's news in that you always hoped for the best, this one coming along to settle her down. After a while, you thought: well, she'll be happy for a year now.

Because she'd be saying: Dennis is perfect.

Luther has qualities I've searched for.

Tucker and I are of the same opinion regarding nuclear war.

Virgil is smart.

Waldo appreciates passion.

But it was different in that, with Liz Taylor, her life is like a comic strip, Steve Canyon or Mary Worth, misleading crooks and kinks of plot dramatic but trivial, the ending always easy to figure. Liz thin: I'll never be fat again. Liz fat, saying: I never wanted to be thin. Liz marrying a rich man. Liz marrying a poor man. But, for me, watching Amelia was like being my neighbor, Beulah, who's had six miscarriages and no babies and each time tries not to get her hopes up but, before she knows it, paints the nursery a new color, sews a layette, picks out yet another name.

With Amelia it was like that.

I wanted her rolling in clover and I never lost the hope.

I've always heard talk that being happy means you're wet behind the ears. Well, I think of Paul Bunyan, the idea that even if you know the wilderness can't be tamed you pretend it can.

How, for instance, if I was a man come to these hills a hundred years ago, facing acres of trees, impediments to my notion of living, which is to say land planted with reliable crops stretching to the west, a snug roof, dry floor, curtains in the window, and I was spending ten hours a day hacking down trees for a way of life I'd never live to see, even if I was not the man but maybe just married to him, I'd spend evenings spinning out tales about a big giant swinging a bad axe and a blue animal hauling trees.

Amelia never understood you live with confusion, don't put it to rout. Orderly things are wild on the inside. The outside of something, a husband for instance, is the opposite of its core.

The bravest man is scared.

A man that's tender toward others only wants tenderness for himself.

Amelia thinks *wishes* come true.

My mother thinks you get what you want, bliss, with *things*.

To understand Number One, Lance, you have to understand Amelia was a flawless baby sister and me so glad to have her, my living doll, curly-headed, with hazel-colored, sleepy-lidded eyes. We lived in a white house, then a gray house next to the church, then for a while in a house in a development called Towering Oaks, but only for a year, then back to a clapboard house by the mill. I have this one picture, Amelia and me sitting on the running board of our father's '53 pickup, black and shiny, RHODIE'S 24 HOUR TOWING painted on the side. Amelia's wearing one of those red, hooded sweatshirts with a zipper and she has autumn leaves all around her ankles, some in her hair, the tilt of her head just so.

I love my own children of course, ten of them.

We'd never have kept Amelia from school but it was the first scrape.

We'd been away, visiting cousins, and when we got back the kids in Amelia's class were sounding out words, reading short sentences, and Amelia, offended, chalked up reading as one of those things like ice skating that, since she couldn't do well, she wouldn't do at all. Every afternoon I had her climb the tree in the front yard, into the crotch of branches where I'd nailed a piece of wood for a desk, and I harangued her until one day she walked in the house and read out loud, first, her primer, cover to cover, then my fifth-grade book and the *Reader's Digest,* tripping on words she wasn't sure she knew and, recognizing them, opening her eyes wide, forging ahead. My father said, "I'll be damned."

He was glad.

Or would have been.

But no one does it for a living, reading. The next eight years is a series of incidents like Amelia drawing her mouth into an inhospitable line, saying: "I never saw a moor, I never saw the sea; Yet know I how the heather looks, and what a wave must be." Or Amelia being yanked from under the bed where she'd been found, not cleaning or studying multiplication, but reading *Bennett Cerf's Book of Laughs,* or the biography of St. Bernadette of Lourdes (we weren't Catholic), or *Gothic Conventions in Great Literature.*

Our mother kept out of it when our father fussed about Amelia's reading, but privately she'd say: "I married down," which is an attitude she got from our grandma who—judging from one photo of our grandpa, him on the roadside with a woman who's wearing furs, the kind with sly heads and feet dangling down like a five-point star, a woman who is not our grandma and sits on a road sign shaped like an arrow that says WADENA 7 MILES, the curve of her butt nearly covering it—well, she married difficulty. She was involved in temperance even after the repeal: lips that touch wine would never touch hers. Grandpa kept liquor in the barn on the pretext, pretexts being what men keep, it was for sick cows.

Winters are long here and suited for not much else.

I've cut Ralph off a few times from love.

I've grown used to the smell of whiskey with it, on Ralph's breath, his skin.

But Amelia is seduced by mystery, an aura suggesting stories to be told.

Lance Greenfield was a towheaded man who couldn't get women his own age. Though I will say he stayed at his father's farm when he was old enough to have a place of his own, not because he was stingy, as people said, but because his dad had heart trouble. Amelia saw him working forty hours a week at the phone company, then home to bail hay and deliver calves, and she thought he was a rube, but innocent, loyal. That's what love is, taking someone's worst quality and making it their best. I've done it with Ralph, seeing his guilt over whomping other women as a change-producing but unchanged substance, the reason by which he felt compelled to build the Towering Gazebo for me, and turn our thirty acres, which he had in mind for a housing development with streets named after our kids, into an arboretum with plaques that say: LO, BIRDS ARE ON THE WING, or HOW WISE THE SAVAGE WHO SEES ETERNITY IN BABBLING STREAMS, or, on the arch above our twisted, mazing driveway, PEACE TO ALL WHO ENTER HERE.

We'd just moved to the woods, to a foundation with plumbing we used for the kitchen and bathroom and Ralph built the bedroom on top, no living room; you can see how I got with child immediately. It looked like a shoe, or boot maybe, and we slept in the ankle and cooked and did our hygiene in the foot. Amelia met Lance and our father fumed, saying what could a man his age want but one thing, then figuring what the hell, she was fourteen. Mother had big plans for Amelia, Normal School, which is what she called teacher's college, but Amelia would say she was at the library or high school planning for a Forensics Tournament, and she'd meet Lance. He'd drop her off later a quarter-mile from home, on his motorcycle in summer or snowmobile in winter, and a neighbor saw and called Mother, who wrung her hands and took Amelia to New Ulm for birth control, a subject she never broached with me.

Amelia married Lance and was concerned with beautification, embroidery, decoupage, stripping and repainting, also books, ideas dressed up. One autumn afternoon she called and said, "I'm coming by to get you because a cow fell in the well hole by the Dove-Cote Cottage." I said: What? She said, "Nadine, the Dove-Cote Cottage." It turns out the Dove-Cote Cottage was what she called the foundation to a sod house that used to stand in old man Greenfield's pasture. When we got there, Lance was worried. The veterinarian climbed down and put a chain around the cow to tow her out with a tractor, and Amelia went on about the stone cellar and the house she'd like to build on top to the extent she was even talking about what size rug she'd put in front of the fireplace.

One of my favorite places to visit is the Museum of Domestic History where they show antique iceboxes, brooms, washing machines, hatpins, baby prams, so on; but Amelia's timing was off.

They drug the cow out and her leg was broken, the bone having punctured the hide from inside to out, showing white, phosphorescent. Her full bag—she'd been missing for two days and not milked—scraped hard against the sharp-edged rock rim. The chain was wedged in what, on a human, would be called the armpits and her front legs were pushed up by it, in overture, it seemed, pitiable. Amelia shrieked and carried on until it was her Lance tended and not the cow. As the vet and I went back to the barn, at dusk, Lance's words in our ears, *Amelia is tenderhearted,* I thought, and I'm sure the vet did too, yes: but to what good? At first she'd made Lance special food and bought him gifts and in the end wouldn't draw a bath for him when he'd come down with a cold. She'd say: that's the third cold this winter. I was there once when winds blew, rain poured, phone lines were down, and Lance called from the top of a pole to say don't worry he wasn't in danger. She looked confused and hung up: she hadn't considered he was.

Let me stress, Lance was the only one who died; he died when his yellow-colored truck left the highway for the third time that winter during which the sheriff wrote *Swerving to avoid a deer* all three times, to avoid writing *Asleep at the wheel,* in which case the insurance company wouldn't have paid. *Asleep at the wheel* is the phrase most of us approved, closer to truth than stories about deer and yet dignified, more polite, not *Drunk again.*

What's in heaven? I remember I thought as I sat in the second row behind Lance's family, his two brothers, their necks swelled, it seemed, because they choked back tears, didn't shed them. Amelia was at the end of the pew. Ralph said at the wake, drunk and not too loud, she was responsible. It served a purpose, all of us having thought it and glad someone said it, but most of us unwilling to be mean or possibly wrong and even Ralph relieved, later, he could wash over it as something whiskey said, not him. I was pregnant again, a pillow propped behind my back on the folding chair, and aware of Ralph's infidelities in a peripheral way, in the way a mother rabbit is, for instance, of danger, its smell. I thought two things: it wasn't fair to blame Amelia for Lance being too weak to say what it was he wanted in a wife and then to insist on it; and, also, that she was still young.

Beulah had her third miscarriage that summer.

I remember. I went to see her. My babies were fat and peppy.

Amelia's "Where the Boys Are" phase began then, when she was a seventeen-year-old widow living in a trailer and working on her General Education diploma. The college-boy social worker who couldn't get a better job and came by to teach her had an afternoon with her. There was the Norton boy, who would have married her and ended up marrying that Habbeshaw woman from the hills; after he said, they were on my porch, "Amelia, every minute with you is pleasure. I'd die if I thought someone else had it." She was lying on her back, her legs across his chest, one bare foot stroking his cheek. A week later she pulled into the gas station he worked at and said, "Fill her up," another man sitting beside her.

And our father met a woman and the secret wouldn't keep, didn't stay an idea, words and gossip, but started being things, places, sounds, smells. One night, his face inflated as though it might burst, he showed up with his girlfriend at a dance at the Armory he knew I'd be at with Ralph, and Amelia, and whoever she happened to be with. He evaporated for Amelia then, like a relative you stop inviting to dinner because he always shows up drunk.

After making threats she didn't mean and he knew it, Mother said let him have his own way and eat it too. But he didn't come home and, when his girlfriend insisted, filed for divorce. So Mother married a man who stayed drunk twenty-three hours a day and sat there, poured out for him, nodded as he talked, the idea being he'd stay.

I had four children by then.

The names for all ten are, the boys,

Randolph

Reginald

Roderick

Rowland

Raphael

Rufus, all of them starting with R to honor Ralph, and the girls,

Nanette

Nellie

Nola and

Nina, to honor me, my name: Nadine.

I love babies, their faces, the way they open wide, sparkle, gesticulate extraordinarily at what's ordinary, a dog, water, branch, cloud, because they're not from here, not local, but dropped out of the sky, bouncing down like hail on the desert, which I've never seen but I imagine is white, unrelentingly hot. Ralph always calls the littlest one The Basketball, a way of describing that curled-up look, the sturdy, round bulk of babies. "Where's The Basketball?" he says, looking around the room, or, "Let's put The Basketball to bed now so we can all get some shut-eye."

Mother's new marriage lasted five years. Then she quit him, started her religion.

Around my fifth baby, who was Nanette, my first girl, on a winter night so cold the snow crunched as tires rolled over it on the highway, we got a call for Ralph to haul a car out of the ditch near the overpass by Wadena, where every year there's accidents, the air above and below the overpass so cold it causes a freezing-over more slick than the rest of the road, and you'll be coming down it break-neck but gripping and all of a sudden the surprise of the ice, whirling you around faster than you'd require for even excitement's sake. People get killed. We never intended for Ralph to work for my dad forever towing cars, the idea being it was steady money until we built the development with streets named Roderick, Nanette, Rowland, Nina, Rufus, so on.

But when, in the business of sleeping, making love, and tending children, do you do this? More important, who would front us the money?

Years passed.

When Ralph had been gone too long that night to have just towed a car, and when I weighed the likelihood of him in that weather in the middle of the night going to whomp the waitress from the Rib Shack against the thought of him in the ditch, pinned, freezing to death, or dying of carbon monoxide, I put my snow-mobile suit on top of my flannel nightgown, also warm boots, a hat, gloves. I drove the VW bus carefully, carefully I thought, having two lives to save, my own and Ralph's. When I got there, the car was hitched to the truck. They saw my approach, lights. It wasn't like I looked in and saw Ralph's butt, his familiar backside, the rise, fall, tremble. The windows were fogged. But when he opened the door and the dome light went on, I didn't recognize her, her tousled hair, her red mouth a slash. Bundled up, nothing to show but my face, my boots clumping, I stalked in the road like a pure alien sent down to show, by contrast, what it means to be more than human. I thought: grief is not being able to say the source of pain is in your head.

With most trouble you say, I won't think about it. And you don't.

It's only worry: saying to yourself, what if . . .

You counter it by saying: what if *not* . . .

But some things won't be pushed away and Ralph was no help, coming to me for six months looking like a child who's broken my best vase or bashed his brother's head accidentally. I'd relive it, saying, well, her hair could have got mussed from the accident, the whirling around. Or: he was letting her warm up before they headed back to town. About the smell that had seemed to me at the time the smell of sex, creamy and rich, like ripe corn, I thought: how reliable is evidence as irretrievable as that?

But Ralph insisted we make love two and three times daily, like it was discontinued, wouldn't be in stock the next time he craved some, even pulling off the road one afternoon we'd left the kids with Amelia and had been to town to buy bulk groceries. I felt the old surge as we drove into lush trees, remembering freedom, that these bowers were what we had when we were young, still living at home. Looking out the window, I remembered the other time Ralph had urgently needed the fact of me to lean against and make love with was the spring his mother died and how he'd used it as a way to lay his head down, and coming, shouting out and breaking all the way down, was what he did instead of cry.

Beulah, my neighbor, says Don, her husband, who'll hardly make love unless she insists, which is when she tries to get pregnant, reaches out for her after the miscarriage when he's grieving, but also exactly, it's sad, when the doctor says she can't.

At home, Amelia was watching the kids with Number Two, Jim Martino, who I appreciated but Ralph couldn't because Jim didn't know the difference between a crankshaft and cam drive and once tried to mount a tire on Amelia's car wrong side facing out. But he was raised by his mother, I'd say, how could he know about cars?

I was pregnant for the sixth time. As we sat down to the table, Amelia complained that the Bookmobile, which came to Wadena every three weeks, wasn't getting new books, and three weeks was a long time to wait anyway. And Lance Greenfield's one brother was coming by the trailer when Jim Martino was at work and staring at Amelia, she said, like she was a ghost, or naked. She wanted to move the trailer to our land to get away from Lance's brother, also to save money so Jim could work at the mill while she went to New Ulm every week, Monday through Friday, to Normal School.

Ralph was chewing his dinner, smiling at the same time. "It won't take," he said.

Amelia enunciates when she talks. "Teaching," she said, "unlike towing cars, does not cause pollution, or overpopulate the earth."

She looked at me.

Ralph said, "I meant they won't make you normal."

That's how he shows he's comfortable with you, giving you grief.

Jim Martino smiled too, until Amelia lashed him with the back of her hand. The story about him is that he grew up in St. Paul and when he was a kid his parents had a bad fight, and his dad moved out to the garage and sat in a vinyl chair eating raw carrots and potatoes from the extra refrigerator. He came inside once in a while and ate meat and gravy too but, the way Amelia tells it, the only time Jim saw his dad was by going to the garage and he'd be sitting there in the dark, crunching. And once he called the police and had Jim arrested for breaking city curfew. The upshot was Jim got the idea early that relations between men, women, and children were havoc-wreaked by city living, and as soon as he was old enough he drifted from small town to small town.

What Amelia liked about him was that he wasn't from here.

What he liked about her was that she was.

I thought this as I said, "You're going to leave Jim alone, then come home on the weekend, clean up after him, and do homework too?"

She said, "That's the other thing. He can eat here."

The phone rang and it was my mother.

The idea of marrying down seems handy to people because they think, at least my mother did, that a low-class husband will be so glad to have a high-class wife he'll always let her have her way, back off and be the Private and meanwhile let her be Sergeant. But my mother's husband got sick of doing everything wrong, signing his name, hammering a nail in, raking leaves, fishing. (Her second time out she hooked a 42-pound bass and got her picture in the *Dickey County Leader*.) So he hadn't been sober for months and a few nights a week he'd rip the cupboard doors off the hinges, tear the avocado green telephone off the wall. And once, when she left dinner for him on the table as he stayed up and drank, he emptied potato salad on her head when she was sleeping.

She said, "Nadine, I know you're too busy with your husband, children, dogs, and cats to care about me, but I wanted to say Amelia's going to Normal School at last, and I know you'll help her any way you can because it's about time we got the family back up to snuff." And she talked about her mother, my grandma, who'd been educated at the University of North Dakota. Amelia was our hope, bright prospect. "Help her," she said, and hung up.

I was mad at Ralph, though neither of us knew it yet.

As I sat down, he was saying, "It's not that I don't want you here, Amelia, it's that clearing a spot for your trailer and having it there will be one more thing to get around, another what-cha-ma-call-it when the time comes to build the housing development."

"Obstacle," Amelia said. "Jim could be manpower." She laid her fork down and tilted her head. "*If* the time comes," she said.

That didn't pester Ralph.

What I said did.

I wish I could claim it was a voice inside me wired up and speaking, like the bold frog in the fairy tale who jumps out of the princess's throat every time she decides to be dainty, polite. But I knew what I was making, insults only a spouse can. I mentioned every dream or scheme, large or small, Ralph ever had, but, no, really, just ones that failed. I talked about the time he'd tried to earn a living selling erasable memo boards you stick on the refrigerator with magnets, the book he wanted to write about the woods being a fine place to rear children because you teach them about life, sex education, pointing at animals for examples. How he'd been to college for two days and quit because he was embarrassed to ask how to find the buildings his classes were in. The time he thought he'd fix the plumbing himself and, for temporary, used a cardboard tube that wrapping paper comes wound on and lined it with plastic. It held for ten minutes, burst, and ruined the dry wall.

Once he fixed the tension on my sewing machine with a rubber band; it still works. I didn't mention that. I said, "Housing development. Ralph Rockefeller, hmmph. A dog house development, maybe."

My parents used to hiss slurs at each other. I imagine my grandparents did.

And I'd seen Amelia too hard on Lance the last year he was alive.

Ralph looked up, red in the face, stirred his food, and said, "I've failed at most things but one thing I did right was marrying Nadine."

He made it impossible for me to ignore the adultery.

Yes that. And he was acting like a nervous, irresolute child.

I cut him off, the first time. I said the doctor had said not to jar the baby (I was seven months along), nonsense and Ralph knew it. But he went to sleep holding my hand. I lay there and remembered how, when I was a girl, and having heard stories about grim forests, trolls who'd lock you up, witch-mothers who'd gnaw your bones, I decided that darkness and fear of it could be obliterated, stopped, if you faced the night not alone but next to someone who wasn't perfect, just well intending. I looked at Ralph, curled like a tame snake beside me, and I didn't feel a thing.

The next day I realized he thought I'd cut him off because I wanted Amelia to move her trailer out to our land. I looked out the second-story window of our odd-shaped house and saw him and Jim Martino swinging axes, their backs bare, flannel shirts tied to their waists. I thought about Paul Bunyan and the story that tells how, after clearing all those trees, he got sick of sunlight and well-ordered rows and moved to the Valley of Echoes, a place so gloomy a snapping twig sounds like a shot thundering from a cannon, and nearby the Cliff of Rolling Stones where no man is safe. That's where he found peace. Sunlight caught the edge of Ralph's blade, thudding up and down, and glinted steely blue.

Amelia and Jim Martino moved their trailer to our land, a precarious arrangement. Three weeks later, she stopped coming home on weekends. Jim would call her number in New Ulm at eleven or twelve on Saturday night, no answer. Except the next day she'd say she'd been at the all-night library, an excuse that seemed fishy even to me, and I've never lived in town. Ralph and I saw the future, Amelia headed toward another husband, Jim Martino dropped off on us like a kid. Next, my mother called on a day with chilly, freezing rain to say her husband had reached a phase of madness so acute she feared for her life. I said, "What exactly did he say?"

She said, "I feel it, danger."

"Did he threaten you?" I said.

She said, "There's a gun in this house, I can tell."

I told her to stay put, to quit coffee, not to have rash ideas. I hung up. One reason I didn't want to rescue her was my father's girlfriend, Carlotta, who he was planning to marry now, a fine woman. I told her once, "I could be in your company every day and never get tired of it." She smiled, squeezed my arm. Dad was looking hale and well fed, bringing presents for my kids, and I knew if Mother came the opposite would happen. Dad and Carlotta would stop coming over and Mother would start her discipline drills. She likes to put something that the kids want, a cookie or a toy, on one side of the room, and say, "Stay, stay . . ." Then: "Okay, get it." Just like Ralph does with the retrievers.

But that night Rowland, who was five, had a bad dream. I took him out of the boys' bunkroom to the living room, which Ralph had just finished that summer, and I paced around and let him look out the windows into the gnarled black branches, outlined with snow. I said, "See, see." And I tried to get him to talk about the dream and have him realize for himself it wasn't true. He twaddled on about how it had been the end of the world and instead of heaven there was a work camp that was beautiful only because the dead people kept it up, raking and hoeing. He'd been trying hard to get back to earth when he woke up, crying.

He fell asleep. I put him to bed and prowled the house. Watching the snow filter down and down, and cover the earth, I thought of Lance, his short life. I picked up my *Good Housekeeping* magazine, thinking stories about black heel marks, white whites, and good toothpaste would drive the night back. But I came across a list of statistics about at-home violence, and an interview with the aunt of a victim who said they'd seen her niece's murder coming but no one had had the good sense to stop it. I made up my mind then, come morning, if Mother still felt she was sitting on a keg of gunpowder, we'd fetch her here. We moved her in the worst weather. She moved home once, then back here. I helped her myself that time because Ralph and Jim Martino wouldn't.

We had Mother in the house, Jim Martino at the trailer, Amelia dropping in now and then with an attitude like Jim was her poor third cousin, someone she hadn't seen in a while and was glad to see now, but at a distance, remote. She was in love with Dennis from New Ulm. "He's perfect," she said. That's what I remember about him, and he was her teacher. He drove a sports car.

When we went shopping in New Ulm for the wedding dress for Number Three, Dennis, I was pregnant with Nellie, a hard, aching time. Amelia spent $800 on a dress, then had the train cut off. She stood on the pedestal in that fitting room which, with its dozens of mirrors, seemed like the inside of a prism. She shimmied, admired her own shoulders, said, "I've never had a picture-perfect wedding. This one's going to be. Dad and that woman aren't welcome." I tried to say that the wedding is what you do for other people, and marriage, what comes after the wedding—all that time she'd have alone with Dennis for the rest of her life or his—that's what you do for yourself. She said, "I think of how he ruined Mother's life, and the dedicated wife she'd been, then tossed away and made to live with a lunatic in a shanty on the edge of town." I thought Amelia was straining a little to make Mother seem like St. Bernadette of Lourdes. And I said so.

She tilted her head, gazed deep into her mirrored eyes, and said, "Well, if she doesn't clean up her act now, she's not welcome either."

I flashed to the truth: that Amelia made stories up about people.

I decided, though the idea bothered me, that the only person she'd love till death did her part was herself. She hummed a song, the blower in the ceiling fluttering her white dress, and it seemed like the woman on her hands and knees with pins in her mouth who was tending Amelia's train was thinking exactly the same thing.

But in the car on the way home I thought how Lance had been a first marriage, and Jim Martino caught her on the rebound, and a man who could afford $800 for a dress was going to be fine, perfect. Then she said two things. First, in spite of Ralph being not-her-type, I had an ideal marriage and nothing could shake her faith in that. And, second, when I said how odd it was Mother had once had a vision her husband kept a gun in the house and then moved back in with him and watched, sure enough, as he pulled one out of a closet and shot holes in the ceiling, Amelia said: "Of course. Feelings become facts as soon as you say them."

Danger Ahead.

That was my feeling.

We moved Mother to the trailer that used to be Amelia's and Jim Martino's, and Jim into the bedroom in the house that had been Mother's. The kids didn't like her. She'd let her hair grow out of its perm into a bush that stood out from her head by several wild-looking inches. She talked about Faith being Belief in Best Possible Outcomes and how you show you have it with Tokens.

Amelia left Dennis to travel with Luther.

She wrote this to me on postcards from Utah, New Mexico, Texas, California. She brought him home to visit, Number Four. He had a mustache as big as a whisk broom and a silver jacket that said, on the back, COWBOY POETRY. This refers to poems that cowboys used to write and people save for museums. Some people, like Luther, who is only a cowboy in that he drifts across the West, still write them. "I'd like to have a range to tame" is a line I remember from one poem which either he wrote or someone famous.

Don't marry him, that was my advice. She wrote back: Too late.

Next, we got pictures from Hawaii. She was wearing flowing dresses and jewelry made from seashells. She was a writer herself, she said, working on a book about ghosts who live in volcanic ashes. Luther was in the pictures too, his mustache more striking than ever since it was the only thing he had on besides swimming trunks. And there was another man in the pictures, Tucker, a photographer who was working with her on the book. He was known for nuclear war protests. Don't marry him, I wrote.

I meant Tucker.

She wrote back: Don't worry.

Ralph was less fussy about who he whomped than before. Either that, or I was more suspicious.

He thought he half solved the problem by always mentioning the powerful man he was, could be. He talked about the housing development as if it was already built. Once, we were paying our bill after eating at the Rib Shack and someone who was sitting at the bar remarked that, from the road, our place looked like an Indian reservation or a junkyard. I stared at the row of faces, stiff and mysterious, from which it was impossible to say who'd said it, for what motive, why men talk the way they do. I said, using for example the development I'd lived in when I was a kid (Towering Oaks, which was going to pot now because it had been built cheap in the first place), that we'd seen the sign of passing times.

"What's that?" an old fart asked.

"Paradise isn't tame," I said. "If you weren't stupid you'd know that."

Ralph's smile twitched. He took the toothpick out of his mouth. "We'll see you boys later," he said. In the parking lot, he asked if I was following in my mother's footsteps—on the ragged side.

I got in the truck and slammed the door. "They don't respect you," I said.

He said, "Sure they do."

I said, "Someone doesn't. I can tell."

That night I applied myself to the problem. One, Ralph whomped around, felt guilty, advertised the fact. Two, he lacked purpose.

One was a cause.

One was a symptom.

I was interested in Mother's idea, tokens, Belief in Best Possible Outcomes. She was in the kitchen with Beulah. Around the time

I'd had Raphael, my seventh child, who'd seemed to me as beautiful as the first, who was also one more baby than Beulah had had miscarriages, Beulah moved in with us. Her husband, Don, stood in our yard a few nights a week and cried. Mother was cooking seeds for Beulah to eat, pumpkin seeds, pomegranate seeds, sunflower seeds, stirring them in walnut oil in a pan Ralph and I had bought when we were first married. The pan was a token, she said, because Ralph and I had babies. Her other advice to Beulah was be around me, do what I did, wear my clothes.

I was looking at my *Good Housekeeping* magazine, at a picture of a bench you make for your garden with bricks and stone. I said, "Mother, how do you know if you're using the right token?"

She said, "A wish is a flimsy thing. Pick something rigid to stand for it."

I also saw pictures of a folly, a screened-in veranda that sits on the riverbank so you see trees, hear frogs and crickets, but don't get bothered by bugs. And carpenter's plans for a powerful structure made of cement and steel beams: the Towering Gazebo.

She said, "Concrete."

I said, "What?"

She said, "Stiff and hard."

Beulah ate seeds.

I set spring for my deadline.

When the subject of the development came up I'd say, to anyone who'd listen, "Ralph thinks it's wrong to chop the forest into lots the size of hankies with tepid ponds and runty trees. We don't want to break the wilderness up, just live in it." And I'd talk about Paul Bunyan, his mistake: clearing trees, then wanting them back. Remembering Luther, I'd say cowboys had spent the first century making badlands safe and the next wishing they hadn't. I'd think of Ralph: how just a little tame I wanted him, not thumbed-under like Amelia's husbands. Guilt had him acting like that.

"We're building an arboretum," I'd say. It was an idea I got from my research: a place for the exhibition of trees. At first, Ralph was confused. But soon he nodded his head, and after a while he thought it was his idea. He'd repeat my speech about cowboys and Paul Bunyan, adding to it ideas about the woods being a fine place to rear children, how we were going to let Boy Scout troops and 4-H clubs tour it, the rocks and steel beams we had stockpiled now, the nature trails named after our kids. And we were over the hump, I thought, out of the woods by staying in them.

By winter, the frame for the Towering Gazebo stood black and inflexible against the sky. The folly on the riverbank was done, an odd place to visit with its false feeling of shelter, snow having drifted through the windows across the floor and into the fireplace, the latch on the screen door jammed with ice. Jim Martino quit the mill after taking a class on how to carve tombstones and set up shop on the east end of our land and began the plaques which put into words our feelings about life, how to live it.

Amelia called from Santa Ana, California.

Ralph and I had been on the porch off the second story of our house, bundled up, surveying the year's work, our breath hanging in white clouds around us like the bubbles in comic strips which tell what characters think. We decided we'd have to quit until the weather let up. I meant not to sound uneasy, but I was. Amelia noticed when I picked up the phone, but she didn't dwell on it, stuck on her own trouble, which was that she wanted to leave Luther for Tucker and Luther wouldn't let her. She said, "I don't understand. I've always seen Luther as a peaceful man."

I had too, but because she'd said so.

I tried to talk her into sticking it out with Luther, who, in my mind at least, I'd grown to like, his worried face, his mustache which always put me in mind of a pig's bristle scrub brush. She said, "No, politically we're incompatible. I'm coming home."

I tried to talk her out of that, with the twins, Nola and Nina, my eighth and ninth, being newborn, taking up time. I said, "If you're leaving Luther to marry Tucker, what about Tucker?"

She said, "He's coming too."

We had nine children, dogs, cats, Beulah, Mother, Jim Martino, but not much room.

I said so.

She said, "Get rid of Beulah and Jim Martino."

We picked her up at the bus depot in New Ulm two days later, also Tucker, who was shivering, wearing a silver hoop in one ear which conducted the cold, he said, and made the right side of his face feel frozen. He called Amelia a name—Bakkha—someone she used to be, he said, in another life. She rushed off the bus, her hair flying, jewelry clacking, and said, "Where are the children?" She looked at them, then blinked. She said, "The babies?"

She always thinks she wants to hold a baby, then does, frowns, hands it back to me.

Nola and Nina, because they're twins, were especially tiny and wise-looking, sly, more than ever likely to make you think they're not from here, or us, not ours at all. I pulled the blanket back from the pram to show her. She said, "Where's the car?"

On the way to it, she pointed at Jim and said, "Why is he here?"

(He doesn't love you, was one answer I had. *You're not worth straw.*)

"Ralph likes him," I said.

I decided it was annoyance I felt: small rage. I pictured it, coals, gray and cool-seeming on top, but underneath, red and hot.

We stopped at a mall so Ralph could take Amelia and Tucker to a store to buy warm clothes. Jim Martino ran down the mall with Randolph, Reginald, Roderick, Rowland, and Nanette, and I stood in front of a drugstore with the youngest kids. I rocked the pram back and forth and Raphael and Nellie showed me pictures they'd drawn of the Greyhound bus Amelia had come on. That's when I looked up and saw the tabloid cover: Liz Taylor, as big as a house in a gaudy red-and-yellow dress. And I remembered how she used to call Richard Burton *Taffy* and he'd call her *Ocean*, and now she was standing next to a fat man in a bowling shirt, with a caption that said, DON'T MARRY THAT PENNILESS BUM, MALCOLM FORBES TELLS LIZ. In small print: It's Real Love This Time, She Says.

I took Raphael's crayon and scribbled her face out.

On the way home, Amelia asked if I'd throw an engagement party.

Tucker said, "We have a spiritual union."

Ralph said, "Good. Then we'll invite ghosts." He thought it was funny, Jim Martino too.

But I was vexed. On the other hand, I thought what Ann Landers would say: Don't expect the marriage to last without family support.

"We'll do it," I said.

I kept the guest list small:

Ralph,

me,

our children, nine of them,

Amelia,

Tucker (Number Five),

Jim Martino,

Mother,

Dad and Carlotta,

Beulah,

Beulah's husband (Don).

First, I had to clear it with Beulah.

She said, "I won't have Don here. I don't love him. I never did."

Amelia was looking out the window at Jim Martino, who was chopping wood. She said, "I know how you feel, Beulah. But time heals it."

Beulah smiled. "You've always been sweet."

Convincing Mother that Dad and Carlotta should come was harder. She said: No. She said it several times, used my cake decorating kit to write it on the cake (No) when it should have said: Best Wishes. I refrosted it. Next, she flattened one of the boys' toy cars, a Buick LeSabre, with a hammer. I wondered why, then remembered my dad had brought the car over for the boys, a miniature of his own; he got it from the dealer when he bought his.

Amelia said, "What is it with Mother?"

I said, "Her religion." It seemed muddled now, not hopeful. We'd just found a female rag doll, stabbed in the heart with a toothpick, hanging by her red hair from a tree. Carlotta has red hair.

Amelia said, "Does anyone else around here believe it?"

I said, "Of course not."

Amelia said, "Well, Nadine, there's idiots living here. Does Jim Martino pay attention to her, or Ralph? How about the kids?"

I said, "No."

She said, "Or Beulah?"

I said, "Just a little."

"Anyone else?" she asked.

"Of course not," I said. "Who?"

People started to arrive; I served dinner. Dad and Carlotta tried to make conversation with Amelia, who snubbed them. She was cool to Mother, who only spoke to me and Beulah. Beulah didn't talk to Don, who Ralph and Jim Martino felt so bad for that, even though they like to harass him, they asked about his business, the Sport Shop, his gun sales, the price of eels, so on.

That's when one of the older kids told me there was a man in the yard.

It was twilight.

I looked out the window. Against the silver snow of the packed-down driveway, the white and pink-streaked sky, I saw Luther, his mustache frosted up and—I didn't understand why—he was wearing his jacket inside out. I told Randolph to ask him in.

Amelia said, "The effect will be catastrophic."

Mother leaned close. "Ideas," she said, "and not enough things."

Beulah nodded.

Tucker said, "For Christ's sake, Bakkha, let him in."

Ralph opened the door and Luther came charging in, headed for Tucker, and decked him, first with his hand. Then he picked up a stool we'd made when we were first married by covering a 5-gallon steel barrel with foam and vinyl. Any of us could have stopped it sooner, but we froze and watched while the stool went up and down and Tucker's head turned red, unfamiliar. When I finally had the sense to act, I hauled the children out of the room, murmuring something as I did that convinced only the toddlers. I stayed in the bunkroom for a while, reading, acting out skits in a cheerful way. But maybe only five minutes had passed.

Because when I went back to the living room, Jim Martino was pulling Luther off Tucker. "Settle down," he said, "no woman is worth it."

Ralph was holding a towel on Tucker's head. He said, "Some are, but not Amelia."

She kneeled next to Ralph, with Tucker's head in her lap. She said, "I don't understand why someone I love would do this." It wasn't clear whether she meant she loved Luther: so how could he hit Tucker? Or how could Tucker, who she loved, lie there and bleed?

Tucker said, "I didn't fight back, Bakkha, because I can't."

She said, "Of course not, you, you . . . Pacifist," she said suddenly. She bent down, her hair draping over him like a curtain.

Ralph stood up. "Someone take him in for stitches," he said. "Let's clean this mess up. I'd like to eat my dinner." He looked at Luther, who looked miserable and spent. "He needs whiskey," he said.

I left Dad and Carlotta in charge of dinner, which made Mother mad, and she stomped back to her trailer saying I'd taken the notion of Peace too far, by which she meant to refer, I think, to the plaque we'd put up the day before: PEACE TO ALL WHO ENTER HERE. She said, "Lording it over us all the time with an iron hand, queen for a day on a high horse. We'll see about that."

I took these remarks to heart, though I shouldn't have, but when she speaks it sometimes matters that she used to be the person I trusted most. I remembered the first time I'd realized she was talking nonsense and passing it off as wisdom; I was fifteen and we'd read in the paper that someone had drowned and Mother said you don't need to swim not to drown, just hold your breath because it puffs your lungs out like a life jacket and you drown only if you let the air out. I knew it wasn't true if only because once, as a kid, I'd thought that might work and tried it and failed, sunk. And I recalled all the other pithy ideas she'd passed on to me and understood in a flash that she was crazy. I felt sick and tender, and I've felt that way about her since. What she said about me, my high horse, rankled, like she knew my secret: that I had too much power and was trying to give Ralph some.

I looked up and saw Beulah smiling at Don, a milestone, I thought.

I said, "Ralph, be sure to tend carefully to the children while I bring Amelia and Tucker to town so he can get his head fixed."

In the Emergency Room, Amelia petted Tucker like it would numb him. They stitched him up. To ease herself, she made a speech which reminded me of the Forensics Tournaments she used to be good at; and that was because, I think, she was talking to me but staring at the doctor like he was a judge, and it distracted him—I thought for a minute he'd be Number Five, or Six—and she said: "Do you remember that song, Nadine, 'Baby the Rain Must Fall'? I never believed it. What I want from life is perfection. That doesn't seem like much to ask now. Not with the childhood I've had."

It was the first I'd heard of the idea of a bad childhood. But it comes up a lot, I've noticed since.

She said, "I believe in vision, desire. What makes it real?"

The doctor put the last stitch in. "Expect some pain," he said, "and keep it clean."

We went home and she put Tucker to bed and got in with him

to croon. It reminded me of how she'd tended Lance Greenfield the first year. I fed the twins, then put them back down.

I figured someone had driven Luther to a motel or to New Ulm to the depot, and that Ralph was nearby because he wouldn't walk off far and leave the newborns. I settled in my chair in the kitchen in front of the window with a feeling of ease, and it started to snow, and I watched the big flakes fluttering down like moths in the circle of light the yard lamp makes over the driveway. I picked up my broom in that fit of whim I sometimes get, and put on my coat and boots and went to sweep the glassy snow off the paths and sidewalks. I was out there dusting, dusting, and someone clumped up behind me and—with the smell of wind-whipped skin as my cue, and whiskey—I turned around to kiss Ralph.

"Then you feel the same way. My love. Nadine."

It was Jim Martino.

He fell because I pushed him. I swept harder, and fast. "If you can't act decent," I said, "you'll get a place of your own." I wasn't mad, just sapped, the sparkle gone from the night.

He went to the house to sleep it off.

I thought I heard voices from the riverbank. I walked down in the pitch night and stood by the folly and listened to this:

"It's an empire you're making here."

"We want to preserve the forest."

(Then something I couldn't hear well, the *swish*, nylon jackets, one against one.)

"No, no."

"Please, please."

"It makes me feel like a man that you've asked, but, no."

I waited for a minute, doubting. Then I rushed in with my broom and hit the first thing I ran into—Beulah—and I chased her through the woods, slapping her, and down the driveway which seemed to me at the time lit for that purpose: big rage. I pictured it, a soap, temporary purification guaranteed. I turned around.

"I was trying to find a way to let her down easy," Ralph said.

I looked up and saw Amelia staring at us from an upstairs window in her white nightgown, like an angel or saint, I thought. I threw a snow-chunk. It exploded on the glass like a star.

A stone bench is something you can sit on. I've thought this since, as a way to separate my plan to save Ralph from himself, his weakness, from Mother's plan: her religion by which a bench, toy car, rag doll, or a pan of seeds has power. Which is not much different from Amelia's plan: waiting, wishing. Virgil, Number Six, who she married after Tucker, was smart, but if you contradicted him, his calm surface burst and you saw inside, what he stifled: the fear that he was stupid. Thin-Skinned we called him. And Number Seven, Waldo, appreciated passion, she thought, but turned out to have used it only as a way to make her love him, to take him as her spouse and helpmate; after the wedding he never wanted to make love, just someone to eat with him, to go for a drive, to hold his hand during TV football games, and that was it.

The reason she left Tucker, she said, was because she thought he was sure about politics, the way the world should be, but it turned out he'd never thought about it, got the ideas he had from someone else. She called me from Prescott, Arizona. She said, "I'm leaving him. That's the third nuclear war protest this year."

Nothing's pure. I think this.

You go crazy if you worry about dirt, crumbs, dust, bugs in paradise.

Amelia's childhood, as she said, might be the source of trouble, but I also think, having found her books the other day—the biography of St. Bernadette of Lourdes, *Gothic Conventions in Great Literature,* the *Book of Laughs*—that she could have laughed more.

She lives in Bowbells, North Dakota, now, has erased the memory of seven husbands by returning to her *nee* name, Rhodie. She teaches at the high school; once, Ralph asked how she got the job if she never finished Normal School. She can't stand him since the night I hit Beulah with a broom. She said: "Nadine, tell Ralph a diploma is a thing, but I have a unique talent for instilling students with a passion for poetry, a means of finding an ordered world." It was when I found out she was teaching without a diploma that I flashed to the idea that, maybe, in the course of seven marriages and divorces, not all of them were legal.

Do I worry about it?

No.

Mother and Beulah lived together in the trailer, then fought.

Beulah moved back with Don.

I fended off Jim Martino a few more times in the years after that winter night I accidentally kissed him. Once he crouched on the floor and hugged my knees—he was drunk—and called me a fertile goddess. Nonsense, I thought: where does he get it? And I remembered he was raised in the city. He's married to a girl from Wadena now, Sally Norton, and they live above the tombstone shop.

Mother said about Amelia: she's a fart in a whirlwind.

That's her way of saying Amelia blows everywhere, comes to nothing.

As for trouble between Ralph and me, I took *things,* added to them *wishes.*

The arboretum was written up in the St. Paul newspaper with pictures of Ralph leaning against the black tow truck with the white letters RHODIE'S 24 HOUR TOWING and the Towering Gazebo looming behind. During the interview, Ralph said that we have a fine life, getting income from preserving the wilderness, which we'd do anyway, and that we have the family towing business, but only for sentimental reasons, because my dad had begged him to take it.

The interviewer asked how we got interested in conservation.

Ralph said: What?

The interviewer said: Conservation.

Ralph scratched his head.

I said, "Well, it was after we thought about the Paul Bunyan stories."

Ralph smiled. "It was Nadine's idea," he said.

Then the interviewer asked what I thought of our life in the woods.

I couldn't explain.

I thought about it. I considered how it had been, the years I couldn't trust Ralph and it didn't matter, and the years after, when it did, my grief.

The final time I'd cut him off—after I found him in the folly with Beulah—lasted too long, three years, which was why my last baby, Rufus, came so late. And I laid in bed one night and realized that even though Ralph wasn't going around with other women now I'd lost my temper a long time ago and hadn't found it yet. But cutting him off was at cross-purposes; I knew it, remembering my grandma who'd said to my grandpa, You can't have liquor, so he spent all of his time in the barn. And the logic extended to say that if Ralph didn't get love he'd look for it and, like my dad with Carlotta, find it. This scared me, and I went to take a hot shower and when I came back, flopped down, and rolled over, my hair, which was long and wet, landed on Ralph's back: WHOMP.

He sat up, sleepy. "What, Nadine?"

I jacked my head: WHOMP.

I whipped him until he cried. Then I lifted up my nightgown and we made love.

In the morning he said it was the closest we'd been, and he hoped a new baby was coming, a girl, and we'd give it an *N* name, for me.

But it was a boy and we named him Rufus. He's beautiful, roly-poly, fat as a sausage, with the wisdom in his face all babies have until they turn to children, small adults.

I thought this as I held him in the topmost story of the Towering Gazebo one late afternoon and admired the light, the color of harvest in the trees, the rich smell. I remembered the fall afternoon twelve years before, when I'd sat with Amelia and watched Lance Greenfield and the veterinarian pull the sick cow from the well hole, and the pain in Lance's face as he tried to take care of Amelia and the cow too. He never lived long enough to get tenderness for himself, removed in the span of a minute, converted to dust. And I decided that what was wrong with the idea of being dead was that it seemed like living in a desert, dry, unrelieved. I said so out loud as I sat with the baby in my arms in front of the window and stared into the black branches, the orange leaves, dappled, quivering. And he looked up at me and smiled.

Ralph had just come back from a birds-and-the-bees hike in the woods with the older children and they were trooping through the yard with notebooks, butterfly nets, pencils. Ralph called out, "Come in the house, Nadine, and we'll get supper on the table."

I knew what I thought of our life.

I sat there.

And Ralph stood on the second-story porch and said, "Come inside now and we'll put The Basketball to bed so he can get some shut-eye."

A dog barked.

A child called my name.

The sun settled behind a tree and glinted, winked. Heaven.

The Source of Trouble

I was in eighth grade, reading *Teen Beat,* an article called "Double Dare—What To Do When You Accept Two Dates for Saturday Night," and I threw the magazine down on my rib-cord bedspread and looked at myself in the mirror, thinking Geez, counting on my fingers the months until high school, four. My mother says it's short, the time of pale formals covered with net and reinforced with push-up stays that make your cleavage deep, the time between when your date toasts you with his cocktail poured in your shoe and when your husband reads the paper while you pace the floor and the baby pukes. So I hung my red nylon windbreaker over the lamp to make the room dark and I stuck my gum over my teeth to cover my braces, and I thought about how the handyman at school once said to me, "Devita, I think about you every night."

I took my gum off my teeth, put my windbreaker on, picked up my pen and spiral-bound notebook, and went outside and sat on the porch and stared at the lake and made my Popularity Success List Plan: Be nice to boys, all boys, don't make fun of the hair on their chest or legs. Stop saying BALLS. Don't tell that joke about Tarzan's snake being in Jane's cave. Make friends with the smart and pretty girls at Butternut Consolidated High when you go there in the fall, but still be nice to Melissy Smith and Laura Plus (best friends from Glidden).

My mother walked onto the porch and said, "Devita, I got this letter from Butternut High which says you're going to take the tour next week so you'll know your way around in the fall." I threw my notebook down. "I forgot," I said. I'd envisioned myself in short colorful dresses, wearing makeup and heels, my hair long and flowing and boys standing next to their lockers and whistling through their teeth. I'd counted on having all summer to get ready. My mother sat down next to me and stroked my hair. I smelled her Dove soap smell and my love surged. I can't wait until I'm a woman. "I'll kill myself," I said. She said, "We'll order something from Montgomery Wards and it'll be here in time for the tour."

The next day at school, which in Glidden is a one-room building with kids from first to eighth grade, I passed Melissy a note which asked what she was going to wear. She put her hair in her mouth and said, "Depends on what's clean, I guess." So at noon I asked Laura and she said, "Jeans because if you overdress you'll look nervous." I'd considered a blue skirt and blouse with shiny pumps but Laura had a point; I told my mother to order the pale green shorts ensemble with matching sandals.

It turned cold and rainy that day and when I ran down the driveway to fetch the paper wearing my bathrobe and flip-flops, I came back shivering and drenched. My mother said, "Devita, you can't wear the new outfit." We had a fight and by the time Laura's dad was there to pick me up my face was puffy, my nose was running, and I was wearing the shorts outfit but with thick socks and oxford shoes and I had my windbreaker which I planned to ditch. Melissy Smith was wearing a wool dress. Laura wore jeans and sneakers and a sweatshirt that said ANDY'S FISHING LODGE. Genius, I thought: Butternut High is small potatoes, her clothes seemed to say.

We saw the gymnasium, the cafeteria, boys running lathe in shop class, and Mr. Darby dropped us off at the Home Ec room. "Wait here," he said. He came back a few minutes later with two girls. "Del Rae Thomas and Valerie Verholtz live right here in Butternut," he said, "and they're going to be freshmen next fall too." Mr. Darby left, and Del Rae got a box of vanilla wafers out of the cupboard and Valerie turned to us and said, "Have you met the girl from Fifield yet?" Del Rae rolled her eyes and, wiping cookie crumbs off her mouth, pointed at Valerie and said, "Valerie burns."

Valerie said, "I do not."

I said, "What do you mean, burns?"

Mr. Darby opened the door. "This is Bernice Isabell from Fifield," he said.

Bernice was wearing a Schlitz beer T-shirt and a pair of hiphuggers so low they had only three snaps. She smiled and her corner teeth stuck out. Mr. Darby counted us and said, "Okay, that's all the freshmen girls for next year." He shut the door and Del Rae said, "What about you, Bernice? Do you burn?"

Bernice didn't answer.

Del Rae sniffed the air. "Have you heard that theory that if your shampoo and soap and perfume and talcum don't match, and you use them all at the same time, you smell like dog shit?" Bernice put her hands on her hips and stared at Del Rae. Del Rae said, "And some people just roll in it."

Mr. Darby opened the door. "Have you girls made friends yet?" he said. "It's time for the pep rally."

A few weeks later, after school let out in Glidden, Melissy and Laura and I got the same letter, spidery, slant-forward handwriting on notebook paper: A Get Acquainted Before School Starts Next Year Surprise Party for Bernice Isabell, Bring PJs and Blankets. I took it to the living room to show my mother. She was wearing a wide dress with her crackly slip and pouring cocktails. "You drink too much," she said to my father, "and you fall asleep on the couch at eight o'clock."

He said, "I work hard all day, Arla, and I come home and I want to relax."

She said, "I'm sick of it."

I sat down next to my father and smelled him. I love his silky cheeks where he shaves. I showed him the letter. "Why is that familiar," he said, "that name? Oh. They own that tavern in Fifield."

A car pulled up in our driveway. "Arla," he said, "find out who that is and send them away."

My mother opened the door. "It's Jack Burns," she said. Jack Burns lifted her off the floor and twirled her. "Darla," he said. She smiled and straightened her hair. My father stood up and shook Jack's hand. "You're not going to keep us out until dawn drinking and carousing tonight," he said. "I'm tired."

Jack said, "Get me a highball." He smiled at me. "How are you, little girl?" I didn't answer. He said, "Aren't you glad to see me?" Again, I didn't answer. My mother said, "Have some manners, Devita." Jack Burns said, "And after I gave her my swizzle stick collection too."

Laura's dad gave us a ride to Fifield and on the way there I said, "Do you think Bernice is weird?" and Melissy pushed her glasses up her nose and said, "I never thought about it." Laura said, "She is, but Del Rae is mean." Mr. Plus pulled into the parking lot of Isabell's Castle Hill Retreat and pointed at the beer sign. "You girls stay away from the tavern," he said, "you're too young."

He drove away and we stood in the parking lot holding our stuff and no one came so we went inside and a fat lady with piled-up hair who turned out to be Bernice's mom said, "Where did you girls come from?" I said, "We're here for Bernice's Get Acquainted Surprise Party." She said, "Bernice's surprise party?" She wrinkled her nose. "Bernice!" Bernice walked into the barroom and smiled. "Hi," she said. She said to her mother, "I asked some friends over."

We went outside and across this field, and Bernice opened the door to a small house, knotty pine with checked curtains inside. She said, "This used to be where we lived before we built the bar and put the house on top and now I use it for a clubhouse." She opened the top drawer of a dresser. "Look." There were packs of Marlboro cigarettes, a pint of blackberry brandy, all the makeup you'd ever need. I opened a tube of mascara and used the tip of the wire-coil wand to paint a beauty mark on my chin.

Someone knocked at the door. Bernice looked out the window. "Geez," she said, "I can't believe they came."

"Who?" I asked.

She said, "Those bitches from Butternut." Del Rae Thomas and Valerie Verholtz walked in. Del Rae said, "We're here for your surprise party, Bernice." Bernice said, "You know, I was so surprised. I had no idea. My mother planned it, you know."

We started putting on makeup and Bernice got these slips out and said, "These used to be my mom's when she was thin and they look cool with lipstick." She took her T-shirt off and stood there like she wanted us to see her knockers, and she took her jeans off too and put the slip on. She reached in the drawer for a cigarette and lit it and looked at herself in the mirror. "See what I mean?" she said.

A car pulled up. "Well," Valerie Verholtz said, "that's my cue. Good-bye."

"Where's she going?" Laura asked Del Rae.

Del Rae said, "With Rocky, her boyfriend, her parents try to keep them apart, it's so sad. But you know they do burn, I know for sure."

Bernice said, "How do you know?"

Del Rae said, "They did it once when she was on her period."

"How do you know that?" I said.

She said, "I just do. Bernice, do you have some snacks?"

Bernice said, "There's that blackberry brandy and me and Devita will go get food." She tucked her slip into a pair of jeans and put a flannel shirt on, unbuttoned and hanging open. We were walking across the field and stars were twinkling and the grass was cool on my feet. Bernice put her arm around me. "We have a lot in common," she said, "like best friends." She opened the door to the bar and said, "Now get all the beef jerky you can and I'll go for potato chips."

We stood in the doorway and she looked around and her face lit up. "Peanut," she said. A tall guy in a plaid jacket walked over and set his beer down. "Bernice," he said, "you look dandy." Above the V her slip made her chest was delicate and pale. She gave me a quarter. "Play the jukebox," she said.

That's where I met Tim Koofall. He was drinking orange pop and playing pinball while his father drank beer, and it turned out we had the same favorite song: "Gentle on My Mind." Bernice and Peanut were standing in the corner between the bathroom and the pay phone and Bernice's mother yelled, "Peanut, I've talked to you about this before, now get the hell out and don't come back unless you can leave Bernice alone." He left and Bernice walked over and said, "I'm meeting him outside. Forget about the snacks."

In the parking lot Bernice and I stood next to Peanut's Clover Leaf delivery truck and she shoved bags of pretzels under my sweatshirt. "I'll meet you at the house later," she said. I started walking away and the door to the bar opened and Tim Koofall said, "Would you like to go for a walk by the lake?"

We were standing on the pier and looking at the lights on the water, and he told me he was going to be a junior at Butternut High next fall, and he said, "If there was one thing you could change in your life, what would it be?" My hands were in my pockets and I kept my arms close to my sides to keep the snacks in. "I wish my pet rabbit hadn't died," I said. I looked at his profile, and he was wearing a hat with a bill and his nose was one of those fierce-looking ones like I never used to think was handsome. He said, "There's always one incident you can zero down to as the source of trouble and everything bad that happens after it happens because of it."

"An incident?" I said.

He reached for me and the bags of snacks crunched. "What's that noise?" he said. My heart thump-thumped. "Pssst," Bernice said from the bushes. "My mother's on the rampage."

We went back to the house and Del Rae and Laura stood with their hands on their hips. "How dare you leave me here," Laura said. Del Rae said, "I'm starving." Bernice said, "You'll have to wait." She opened the drawer. She reached in my shirt and got the snacks out and threw them in; she ran around picking up cigarettes and ashtrays and lipsticks, and she threw the dresser scarf in too because it had rouge on it. "The blackberry brandy," she said, "where is it?"

Laura handed her the empty bottle. "Melissy drank it," she said.

Bernice's mother walked in as we slid the drawer shut. "There better not be boys here," she said, opening a closet door. "Wasn't there another girl?" No one answered. "Yes," Del Rae said then, "she's sleeping." Bernice's mother walked across the room and pulled the covers back and looked at Melissy. She said, "Does she always wear silver eye shadow to bed?" She leaned closer. "Why are her teeth purple?"

Laura was at my house a few weeks later and we were sitting in the wicker chairs on the porch and she said, "We should keep in mind we're going to have boyfriends soon and we should practice kissing and the things we want to say back when they say they love us."

My parents were in the next room. My mother said, "There's no decent restaurant for three counties." My father said, "So let's stay home." My mother said, "That's hardly the point." She walked away and a door slammed.

"Kiss each other?" I asked Laura. She looked at me. "No," she said, "let's work on our tans." We went down to the boathouse roof, which is flat and overlooks the lake from one direction and the county highway from another. We spread towels and put oil on and laid there, eyes closed, blue-flies buzzing around, and Laura said, "Do you think Melissy is slow?"

I said, "Retarded?"

She said, "About puberty."

Wheels screeched. We sat up. Peanut got out of his Clover Leaf truck. "I thought I recognized you," he said to me. He looked at

Laura and all of a sudden it seemed sleazy that she was wearing a halter. She said, "Who's this?" I said, "Bernice's boyfriend." He said, "Nah, Bernice is like a kid sister to me." He tossed a pack of gum to Laura and said, "How about coming for a boat ride?" I said, "How are we going to tell my parents we're going for a boat ride?" He said, "Meet me at the public landing in fifteen minutes."

Laura walked that half-mile to the landing so fast my feet got scuffed, and Peanut was waiting in the boat. Laura sat down next to him and put her hand on his thigh. He gave her a life jacket. "Don't wear it," he said, "just hang onto it."

I said, "Do we have to jam into these high waves so fast?"

Peanut said, "Have you seen the creek?"

I said, "She has to baby-sit at five."

Peanut slid the rudder to the right, then to the left. Water washed into the boat and suddenly we were in the creek, branches hanging low. He turned the engine off and threw a magazine to me, *The Bass Fisherman*. "I don't feel like reading," I said. He said, "If you wade to shore and walk through the woods for a hundred feet you'll find a road that'll take you home."

I got out and sank to my ankles in mud and when I reached the shore my cutoffs ripped on a brambleberry bush, and I turned around and saw Peanut untying Laura's halter. Sunlight was dribbling down through the trees and her knockers glowed, round and small, pale as snails. "Laura," I said. She said, "What is it?" I said, "If you don't come with me I'll tell." She grabbed her halter and jumped out of the boat. "Balls," she said.

She didn't talk as my father and I drove her home, and she slammed the door when we stopped in front of her house and she got out of the car. My father backed down the driveway and said, "You seem sad, Petunia." I didn't answer. He said, "It's a hard time." I bit my lip and nodded.

"We don't understand her," he said.

"Guess not," I said.

He rubbed his hand through his hair and sighed. "What's her trouble?"

"Who?" I said.

He shook his head and shifted. "It seems like it started as soon as we moved here."

My parents planned my birthday party so they'd take me and my friends across the lake on the pontoon boat to Andy's Fishing Lodge for dinner. Melissy and Laura arrived first and we were standing in the driveway when Del Rae's dad's car pulled up and she got out and handed me a box of donuts. "For breakfast," she said. "We own Thomas Grocery Emporium, you know. Valerie's not coming." She looked at the three of us. "I have the most dastardly secret."

Jack Burns drove up. "Darla," he yelled as he got out of his car.

My father came outside and said, "Jack, we're having a party for Devita but you're welcome to join us." My mother stood in the doorway. My father said, "Arla, it's Jack Burns." She came outside in a white dress with pink palm trees on it and she was wearing pearls. "Wonderful," she said. She smiled.

My father said, "Are we ready?" I said, "Bernice isn't here yet." He said, "The girl from Fifield?" I said, "I'm not going without her." My mother said, "It's supposed to storm so we better go now. We'll leave a note for Bernice on the door."

We were at the lodge eating chicken, and my father and mother and Jack Burns were at the next table, drinking old-fashioneds, and Bernice burst in the door. "Geez," she said, "I hardly made it. Peanut was going to give me a ride and then my mother wouldn't let him, and finally I got a ride with Tim Koofall and his dad." I looked up and saw Tim. He pushed his cap back and smiled. "Happy birthday," he said.

We finished eating and Tim and I took a walk outside and it was dark and he said, "I have this one dream over and over." We stood on the pier by the moored boats and listened to the faraway, tinkly music, and people in the lodge were laughing. Tim jumped onto our pontoon and gave its steering wheel a twist and the night wind blew his hair back, and he said, "I'm walking through these woods and branches scratch me and bugs bite me and it's humid, and I come to a clearing and you're in front of a house with a little rake. That's all," he said, "but I liked it."

"Devita," my mother called.

"I have to go back," I said.

I walked up the path and the music in the lodge stopped, and I opened the door and my father was standing in front of the pinball machine holding Bernice's arm with one hand and Laura's with the other, and they were swinging at each other. "Get the hell out," he yelled at Peanut who was skulking by the side door, "and if I get wind of you poking around fourteen-year-old girls again I'll have you sent up." Peanut got in his truck and drove away, and my father looked at me and shook his head. "And the goddamn Smith girl was trying to get Jack Burns to buy her lime vodka," he said.

My mother said, "It's time to go now."

We walked down to the pier and Bernice said, "I guess I'll ride back to Fifield with Tim Koofall and his dad because I couldn't stand to sleep near Laura." She took off running. "She has a ride home with someone else," I told my mother.

Melissy and Laura and Del Rae and I sat on boat cushions on the front of the pontoon and my father started the engine. Del Rae leaned close and said in a whisper, "Don't tell anyone but Valerie is pregnant and trying to get an abortion, and her parents are Catholic and someone will tell them and she and Rocky will have to get married and I'll be a bridesmaid. That's what I think."

Melissy chewed on her hair. Laura said, "That's interesting."

"You were outside with Tim Koofall," Del Rae said. "It's sad how his father used to be a drunk and then wasn't, and Tim's mother died and his father started drinking again and Tim hardly gets supper now or a place to sleep, and nothing but ugly clothes to wear."

Clouds were rolling across the sky at intervals and in the wake behind us water glimmered. Jack Burns was singing a song about a lady named Mrs. Bliss. "Hush, Jack," my mother said. "As I was saying, my husband and child, their happiness—it's my life."

On the first day of school I was wearing nylons and a new dress and Mr. Darby called us into his office, Laura and Melissy and Bernice and Del Rae and me. We sat in a row. He rubbed his hand over his crew cut and said, "I have something to say."

"It's about Valerie," Del Rae whispered.

He looked at us, his eyebrows wiggly, and he clicked his pencil on the desk. "Valerie Verholtz won't be attending school," he said. "I understand there's going to be a large wedding and many of you will be bridesmaids, punch-servers, whatever. It's an unusual situation for ninth grade and I hope you'll help us maintain a normal atmosphere here. And I urge all of you to make an appointment for the lecture with the school nurse."

A pep rally was going on outside, a bass drum booming, bonfires crackling. Del Rae said, "My father donated those hot dogs." Someone knocked on Mr. Darby's door. "If you'll excuse me," he said. He left the room.

Del Rae turned around. "I talked to Valerie," she said, "and I'm maid of honor and I get to wear a pink dress. Laura and Devita, you're bridesmaids, with pink dresses too. You pass the guestbook, Melissy, and wear a blue dress. Bernice, you can wear anything you want."

Laura said, "A T-shirt. Or, for a formal look, a slip."

Del Rae said, "The dance is at your mother's tavern, Bernice, because no other place would let Valerie or any of us in."

Mr. Darby walked back into the office. "These are precisely the sorts of conversations I hope you'll avoid at school. Now go to the pep rally. Devita, I want to see you." I waited while the others left. He closed the door and folded his arms and sat on the desk. "If something's wrong at home," he said, "we'd like to help."

My father had his suitcase out. "It's a short trip," he said, "and I deserve it." My mother paced the floor and she was wringing her hands. "Our daughter is in the next room putting on her first formal, and for what? Prom? A party? No. A wedding for one of her pregnant school friends. I tell you I won't stay here. If you leave on this trip tonight you'll be surprised when you come home."

I knocked on the doorframe. "How do I look?" I said.

My father's tie was untied. He ran his hand through his hair and smiled. "Like a grown-up," he said.

My mother said, "You should borrow my new earrings, honey." She opened her dresser drawer and I turned to my father and said, "How long will you be gone?" He said, "Not long. You two will be fine." I said, "Will you be fine, Mother?" She waved her rat-tail comb in the air and smiled. "Of course," she said, "I'll curl up with a book."

It rained hard during the wedding, and afterwards we ran down the sidewalk in front of the St. Francis de Sales and got in a car and Rocky's friend, the best man, drove us to Fifield. The jukebox played a waltz, and we drank punch. I said, "Rocky was crying during the vows." Del Rae shrugged. Laura said, "How do we ditch these bouquets so we can dance?"

Tim Koofall tapped me on the shoulder. He was wearing a suit coat and a white shirt. "May I have the honor?" he said. I said, "I don't know how to dance." He said, "Then let me get you a fresh drink."

He walked away and I watched Rocky and Valerie kissing under a paper wedding bell and I thought how she was a woman now, her husband and new-coming baby the center of her life. "Melissy had her first date last night," Laura said, "with the handyman from

Glidden School." Bernice's mother walked past, setting mint cups on tables. "Have you seen Bernice?" I asked Laura and Del Rae.

Laura said, "Let's go to the bathroom."

We went into the bathroom, which is a storage room with a toilet and a sink, and I held Laura's sash off the floor while she peed and I said, "The handyman from Glidden used to have a crush on me." Laura said, "You're not jealous, are you?"

Del Rae said, "You're interested in Tim Koofall now."

Laura said, "I hate his suit coat. What does he talk about?"

I said, "Nothing."

Laura said, "That night at Andy's Fishing Lodge?"

I said, "About a dream he had."

She stood up and looked at herself in the mirror. "His suit coat wouldn't be bad in the dark," she said, "if you were squinting."

"A wet dream," Del Rae said. "Do you know what that is?"

Laura said, "His nose is ugly."

I threw my punch in her face and it ran in pink streams down it, and she blinked and licked her lips. I went outside then and ran around and went down to the lake and stopped in front of the pier and took my sash off and tied it around my head and walked back and forth and thought about Tim's suit, how he just needed a tie. A branch above my head creaked and Bernice slid to the ground. "Geronimo," she said. "I thought you were Laura and I was going to kill you." I said, "I need a ride home."

So I was in the front seat of Peanut's Clover Leaf truck, barreling down the road, and he downshifted and said, "I don't know what it is about you but I've never had the urge." He pulled into my driveway and said, "God, I hope that's not your old man's car." Rain was falling hard and I couldn't see. I fumbled for my key and a single light burned, and I heard my mother singing. I opened the door. She was on the couch in her yellow dress with the ribbons and she was holding a glass.

"Is Dad home?" I said.

She shook her head.

I pointed to some shoes. "Whose are those?" In the next room, the toilet flushed. "Jack Burns," my mother said. He walked in.

My mother said, "Now get out of those wet clothes, Devita, and I'll bring you the hot-water bottle." I went into my bedroom and threw my dress on the floor and got under the blankets and waited for her. I listened to her laughter, its avalanches and slides, Jack Burns's bass echo, ice cubes clinking in glasses and the tall spoon scraping the pitcher. "So free, so free, so free," she said. I thought about my father rubbing his hand in his hair, Tim standing beside me on the pier, the one incident you zero down to, and the wind ripped through trees outside and the light through my window was spastic and my walls swelled and wriggled, and then it was dawn. And Jack Burns got in his car and drove away.

Trouble

Hard luck, it seems, is not a state or even a force but a man or—I'm superstitious—god who changes form, appears everywhere though not, for instance, as a Greyhound bus in town after town, sequentially, but a UFO localizing here, departing suddenly to reappear incongruously faraway, intact, moments later. Omnipresent, omniscient: he knows my habits, exigencies, bruises easiest to make, the old ones, purple, that never heal.

I think this as I stand in a field of wheat, ripe, towering high, on July 4th. Tractors dragging combines cut wide swaths. Farmers sit on top in air-conditioned booths, stereo radio music playing them around, around. "There's no stopping for a holiday when the wheat's ready, it's high summer. The wheat's ready, it's time."

I've heard this talk all week.

Baze, standing next to me, says, "If I were a farmer I'd be conscientious, not lazy, drinking beer." Baze talks this way, as if he had a life once but for some circumstance—losing his leg or manhood, or the IRS got him, or he would have inherited land but an ingrate cousin wiled it away. I'm fed on legends: my stalwart, risk-taking pioneer ancestors; the usual, Paul Revere, Paul Bunyan, God with the capital G who loved the world so much; and the hard-drinking, born-in-water, sprung-from-thighs Greeks. I've been called unique. It's not a compliment. I asked Sherm, Baze's friend, an old man with his own tragic, stagey past (something about his wife dying in a bathtub and they were never sure he didn't drown her), "What is it? What can't Baze live down?"

Sherm looked at me, eyes narrow, spit his tobacco in the can on the floor. "I guess he never figured he'd turn out to be a bum is all."

I say to Baze, "I wish you were a farmer. Think how it would be." This is wrong, I know, the idea that if you could get rid of one factor life would be the same but better, when in fact it would be different but just as bad. Still, it's nice to think of Baze as landed, hardworking, minus that wife he's depicted as teetotaling, Bingo-hopping; seriously, there's only one night a week she doesn't play somewhere, at the VFW, Knights of Columbus, the Masons . . . I've met her. She came in the dispatch office of Shandy's Sand & Gravel where I work, where Baze works. No matter what I said, how many cups of coffee I creamed and sugared, whether or not I asked her how her job at the cafeteria was, she treated me like Baze's mistress, which I am not, though gossip contradicts that.

The sun is red as a tomato, swollen. Ever since I was fourteen and gulped my first wine, more nights than not I'm punch-drunk, intoxicated. I'm careful about the way I lean into Baze now, his forearm brushing against mine, the hairs intermingling, ticklish. How we must look, I think, on the edge of the earth—you can see its curve from here—light bleeding through the seam between us. And I remember something I read last week that said the penchant to dramatize life, to elevate its peaks, stomp hard on the depressions to make them wide and low, was deadly. It mentioned James Dean, Mary Wollstonecraft Shelley who wrote *Frankenstein* and that's about it, Sid Vicious and his sweet moll Nancy.

My father's theory on alcoholism in Russia is that communism is like a garment shrunk too small, hard to wear or live in. He was drinking a fourth glass of warm whiskey as he said this; we were sitting in his living room, trying to talk, both of us, without fighting. His girlfriend, this one looked like Connie Francis, came out of the bedroom in a yellow nightie. What are you doing? she asked, angry at having lain there so long, I guess, ready for love.

"Fighting communism," my father said.

And I laughed. It was a good way to talk about drunkenness, which is what we have in common, besides thick ankles and gray eyes.

"Death to communism."

I raise my peach-fizzed something-or-other in the air as I say this and Baze smiles. He's a restful man to be with because he doesn't ask me to explain things but sometimes says if I didn't think hard I'd be happy, let life flow over me like healing waters, balm.

Baze says, "We should go back."

But I don't want to go back to the party, attended, as it is, by everyone who ever worked for or bought product from the Sand & Gravel, cronies on the one hand, you could call them, or, on the other, not. It's odd how Don Shandy holds sway over not only the men whose checks he signs but clients, as though he'd cut them off from sand and gravel if they didn't act just so and, more eerie, they'd care. Also at the party across the field, three-quarters of a mile away, are the laundromat orphans, the laundromat being the business Don bought Garnett on their twenty-fifth anniversary, the occasion of the only crisis in their marriage, when Garnett was set on leaving because she felt excluded from the steady urgency of life at the gravel pit. She'd worked at the dispatch office, in my position, but they fought in front of the help and that won't do (she'd said), so Don bought the laundromat and they've been happy since.

That's how I met these people, sudsing it up one day at Garnett's, changing out of my dirty clothes in the bathroom into ones fresh from the dryer so I could wash everything and walk away clean, no bundle to lug; generally, I'd rather throw soiled things out than revive them. Of course Garnett noticed, the laundromat being an excuse for her to look after people, her kids grown now, and she tricked the story out: how I was left high-dry and broken down. That's not it, though. I'd walked away from the bastard one morning when he was fixing furnaces and air conditioners at the Army base, the job he thought so great he talked about our future, a house to settle in, how kids should act. (You should write a book, I'd said, thinking of *Child Rearing According to Morons* as a title.) What's in it for me? I wondered. So I took the grocery money and ran.

But Garnett, for reasons of her own, had an alternative story in mind, and she'd waited a long time to displace it. I infer this by how quickly she fitted it for me, pinned its more comprehensive tenor over the sparse details I was willing to provide: ". . . Yes, I'm staying at the Sandman Motel but need to find work or I can't afford it, it's expensive. Yes, it was trouble at home, we weren't married, right or wrong, but it does make splitting up simple . . ."

And I started to see myself through Garnett's eyes—frail, well meaning, a settling-down kind of woman who'd mated wrong. How free I felt of the past then, and shame, a feeling that gets palmed off as good for you, signifying morality, violated, yes, but nevertheless present, a yardstick. Another advantage is play: you don't get bored if you escape yourself. And so I found myself folding bath towels, saying to Garnett, "Well, weeks passed and I realized I would never be happy there, nothing would change, so I pulled myself up by my bootstraps and said: Eve, this is your life, fix it."

This is true of course.

Garnett said, "Was it the same kind of trouble over and over, repeatedly?"

He was the umpteenth man I'd tried to settle on but that wasn't what she meant.

"Yes," I said.

She said, "You were right to leave. You think they grow out of it but they don't. You're young enough to find a man who'll treat you good."

And she got me the job at the gravel pit where I'm the only woman on the premises, bookkeeper, dispatcher, the person who serves beer out of the keg in the office refrigerator at five when the crew comes in. Don Shandy made his passes at me but I gauged the situation right, acted delicate, daughterly, opened my eyes wide when I said things like "You don't think, come fall, I'll have a problem with mice?" (It's one of Don's houses I rent.) He said, "Honey, if you do, we'll send someone out." Once I said, "My car is making a noise like ka-clunkety ka-clunkety, and I hope it's not too expensive." He got someone to fix it and, better, stopped putting his hand on my hip when he talked about Accounts Receivable.

I tell this to Baze as we walk back to the party and he laughs, thinks it's a good joke, says again I know more about the internal combustion engine than any woman he's met. Last week, together, we put an oil-sending unit on my car and he asked me how I got smart about gaskets, wrenches, valve covers. I told him about my father's store, Parts Unlimited, my first job in the office there, concrete walls so thick you couldn't get much of a radio signal through them, a distributor cap on my desk for a pen rack, invoices dusty and grease-smeared. Those summers are linked for me with the lyrics of a song which, I guess, got played a lot back then:

> . . . Though the wheat fields and the coal mines and the junk yards come between us, and some other woman crying to her mother 'cause I left her . . .

The man in it goes on to say that, despite obstacles, the serial barriers he raises up between him and his woman, she has the gift, gentleness, also the foresight to leave his sleeping bag rolled up and stashed behind her couch, a detail suggesting, in a naive but typically AM radio way, that they don't have sex. Yet how I wanted to be like that, a stasis, a pool to dive into again and again.

No one has ever called time spent with me *calm*.

I've resigned myself to that, think instead I'm the minstrel, the stray, wandering electrical current waiting for a tower to discharge on. I tell Baze I developed my theory of life in part because of my father's auto parts store and the used car lot behind. "I got the idea," I say, "that everything could be fixed unless it was totalled, and that doesn't happen much, and small problems get solved with spare parts you buy off someone cheap and install with a slap and flourish. It stands to reason that if you spend more time working on it than driving it, you trade it in and the new one's got problems too, and you take a while figuring out what they are and how to baby it along, but hope, in the end, it's better."

He says, "You think too much."

"Maybe."

But in my mind I add, to all those cars, the progression of women my father dragged through my life, beginning with my mother, brown-eyed, of whom I have only transient memories, the smell of soap, a flashy smile, a visual memory perhaps after all of only a photograph. And the one who looked like Teresa Brewer or tried to, and Doris Day, and more. When I was in grade school, he sent me away every summer to my grandfather's in Idaho so he could live his life more fully. (*Balls out* is an expression a friend of mine uses for people who dance on tables, swim naked at midnight, see monogamy as an ideal, nothing else.) Well, my grandfather had four wives himself, they all died, and each time he moved their clothes and pictures down to the pressed-wood lined basement room I stayed in. On the dresser were photographs of four women, hairstyles according to the era, varying intensities of lipstick, and beside them, I still don't understand, piles of plastic flowers.

I tell Baze about the flowers, the smell of mothballs, how my grandfather liked sausage and that's what we ate. The only other kid nearby was Debbie Hiney, who had a lump on her ear, and all we had in common was hating orange popsicles. The water tasted bad, rusty. I lay in bed on quiet, muggy nights and wished for something else, to eat, to go to, to do. Baze says, "You're making this up, lines of cars, your father's girlfriends, wives for your granddad."

I'm not. I say so. "I'm looking for a pattern," I tell Baze.

He says, "I'd say too hard."

I don't tell him about the dream, yellow buses, me standing on the corner, arms flailing. One has gone past that I missed, I know, and though all the others coming by would take me somewhere, I wait for the first one which, people tell me, won't return so flex your arm, opt for a new destination; I don't. The other repeating dream is about a dark-haired woman who I beat, saying each time my fist meets her flesh: I've stood this, you pushing me so far. This is hard to reconcile with the watery, paperback novel sorts of emotions that, for years, I've cultivated about my mother, and the attendant fantasy that she was angelic, dressed in white, my father a mustachioed villain who drove her over the edge.

Actually, she was behind the wheel and there's no evidence she was anything but glad to be herself, glamorous, married to a smooth-talker.

But the notion that she wasn't has everything to do with why— though in other opportunities I've had to prove myself, I'm a slut —I've never slept with a married man. That makes me a virgin with Baze. And, despite the thirty lovers behind me, which brings to mind another country song, "I can feel you but I just can't find you . . . ," I've always felt pure after taking my months off between lovers, like a bride laid out on a brass bed for the first time. Only once did I make love to more than one man in the same month and even then I noticed the illusion, like a woman with it, is damn easy.

I say this aloud to Baze and he frowns, begins his speech about "That's the third time this week I've heard you put yourself down and I wish you'd stop," not realizing he does it to himself too. We're back at the party now and there's no more chance to talk as we split apart and act as if we wandered accidentally into each other's paths as we were off in the wheat, peeing, as though it's no more important for us to see each other, to talk to, to smile at, than, for instance, Don or Garnett. Or Sherm over there, eyeing us. Or the redhead who left her GI husband and is surrounded now, rejoicingly, by truck drivers. She waves.

Or any of the rest.

I think about it being a family holiday. Baze's wife: where is she, at home, at bingo? He must have felt tender for her once or he wouldn't have married her. Whenever I say this, he gets exasperated, pushes his hat back, says, "I honestly don't remember."

I get myself another drink and Sherm wanders over in blue-jeans, boots (even in this heat), a brown-checked shirt, his eyes squinty behind thick glasses. "Nice evening for a walk," he says.

I say, "Yes, my favorite time of year, the cicada . . ."

I notice Don Shandy staring, not as though he wants me, but interested, invested, like he's made a bet. And maybe he has, the situation prime: a hen in a crowded rooster house as the adage, reversed, would have it. If he did bet, I wonder, what are the terms? That I'd get laid by midnight? By the end of the summer? Are there odds—high money on dark horses—regarding who I'll pick?

Don walks over, puts his arm around me, says, "Baze is a fine fellow who got himself in a fix, that wife. A bad woman can ruin a man."

I'm sure he believes the opposite, that a good woman can save him.

I don't, it irritates me.

("Who can find a virtuous woman? for her price *is* far above rubies.")

I say this out loud.

Don says, "Damn right, go to it." He slaps my ass and walks away.

I like the idea of a Bible, I think, book of wisdom, but every time I sit down and read it I get pissed off. I look around the party, at Baze, his face showing he's worried that Don's pushed too far with me. Baze isn't fine-looking in the way that makes you sigh. I learned a long time ago what handsome men are, catered to their whole lives by, first, parents, next, old maid schoolteachers, next, women, women increasingly young as years go by. I smile at Baze, the way he girds himself in clothes (his uniform: jeans, belt, boots, hat), shy maybe, but I like to think there's a surprise underneath, violent, too ribald or sought after for just anyone.

It's been months.

I'd like to keep it that way, my life: no ornament.

Then I remember the night we pulled off I-70. We'd been down the highway, to McFarland, to a roadhouse. That afternoon, at the office, Garnett had sat me down to get at what she called the bottom of it, this talk about Baze and me. I told her I liked him, there wasn't more to it than that because I had a rule against married men. She patted my shoulder—she's a soft woman, her brunette, gray-streaked hair piled high, eyes mellow behind the rhinestone-starred cat's-eye glasses she wears. I was sitting down, she was standing up. She pushed my head against her stomach, a hug, and said, "That's what I told Don. You're too good a girl."

That was Friday afternoon. Then the crew came in, drank beer, and, an hour later, left. Understand, Baze wasn't worried for himself; I know, from talking to Sherm, he had an affair before and his wife was glad, relieved. But when I wanted to leave my car at the Sand & Gravel, Baze said, "Anyone driving past will see and, come Monday, spread talk." So I drove home, changed into my favorite dress, deep ocean green with pink flowers, white sandals, a pair of dangle-down earrings that looked pearly, like chunks of ice. When Baze pulled into my yard, I rushed out before anyone saw (I live on a stretch of road that runs past the gravel pit), and we headed out, high up in the jacked-up pickup, over hills, down into valleys, lush pockets of cold air, crickets chirping hard.

At the Turtle Dove, in McFarland, he told me about the woman who ran it, the place she used to have in Topeka, the depraved times those were and what they led to: a shooting, manslaughter. "Because he premeditated it ten minutes instead of ten days," Baze

said. "They shut the place down then. Good thing, wild crowd.
I'd had enough."

"This was before or after you were married?" I said.

He thought a long time before answering:

"Before."

"When did you join the Army?"

He thought again:

"After."

Baze has these gaps.

I don't like it.

But soon we were picking out jukebox songs, sitting close. I
love the inside of bars, the salty smell, blue signs revolving with
canoes, white bears, the promise of water. But something happened as we drove home, I can't explain, like having a rheumy
feeling in my elbow that says rain and meanwhile the sun shines.
Well, the moon shone, the air smelled good, and I thought about
my grandpa's wife who walked into town to get him because he'd
left days before to sell the crops and when she found him the
money was gone. I get this confused with a story about my great-
grandma who got so lonesome for kin she walked two months to
visit them, picking up sheep chips on the way for fuel to sell for
bed and board.

The night shut down and I felt Monday coming.

Baze pulled into a truckstop, the edge of it.

Walking inside to the bathrooms, I looked at the big rigs; I've
seen myself behind the wheel of one, rolling, gathering nothing.

As I got back in the truck I saw how the flickering overhead
lights shining through the bug-splashed windshield were making
Baze's skin seem green, flecked. I remembered a story about my
dad who, they say, went AWOL in Korea by jumping in shark-
infested waters and swimming. I shut my eyes, pretended the
sound of traffic on the interstate was waves crashing, and, picturing Baze beside me, extraordinary, said I wanted the lovemaking

to start. He said, "I don't think you do." I said, "Please, I'm tired of waiting."

He put the truck in gear and drove away.

He's never brought it up since.

Sherm places a lawn chair next to mine and sits in it. I see Baze moving through the dusk, his white cowboy shirt a flag, signal.

The fireworks start: that is, faraway, the city display is in striking force, splintery fireballs rolling at me, and over. In front, an amateur show versus a class act, Don Shandy and others light theirs: fizzling, premature. They fly up, sputter, sink. "Light my wick," Don says then and, harking to the sound of it, the opportunity for bald metaphor, he throws the firecracker down, holds his crotch, yells, "How painful." Anything sets him off, talk of dipsticks, woodpeckers, breed bulls. Once he refused to eat a hot dog on a stick, saying, "It makes me feel strange, seriously."

In the midst of this banging around and hijinks, Sherm says, his voice quiet, "Right or wrong, I don't presume to know the difference, too complicated."

I say, "Are you talking to me?"

Another firecracker whistles and bursts.

Sherm says, "Love is a direction."

But like what: east, west, a tug?

Or How To ("For success do this, next this, and, finally, this . . .")?

He says, "We don't get many and my feeling is follow it."

The fireworks end.

I pack up my coat, shoes, the casserole dish with my name on it: Eve Hackanson. Baze walks over, hands in his pockets. It irritates me: lazy, complacent, sure. When I don't speak, don't rush in with some observation about patriotism, mineral particles bursting in air and fouling it, Baze clears his throat, says: "Heading out?"

His best try.

Or a way to disguise facility, the language (seduction) being his first.

I say, "Would you like to come over?"

Baze wonders aloud where to park his truck so people driving past won't see the spectacle, big machine in my driveway as sexual as the glow of light from my upstairs window. This is a paraphrase.

I say, "Take a chance or don't."

(Heroes, see COURAGE, aren't false.)

He says, "In about five minutes."

I drive home on the road turned ink-colored by the night's light:

> The road was a gypsy's ribbon, looping the purple moor,
> And the highwayman came riding—
> Riding—
> Up to the old inn-door.

I say these lines as I crest small hills, remembering the old poem as I do, the landlord's daughter letting her hair hang from the window and he kisses it ("o, sweet black waves in the moonlight"). She saves him from enemies by shooting herself. I gave a report on it in school, saying he was a criminal and she saw good in his heart and kept the police from taking him. The teacher stopped me, explained: he was the patriot and the people she saved him from were crooks. The teacher said: Eve, you confuse protagonists with villains.

At home, I turn a fan on, make sweet drinks.

Baze comes in.

There's no way to dim the lights so we sit on edge of the couch, blinking.

He looks at a book I've left lying spread-eagle on the floor: *The World We Have Lost.*

I tell him I understand most of it, not all.

He says, "Ignorance is Bliss."

It isn't a joke.

I ask him about Sherm, the stories I've heard. He says, "His wife was beautiful but a whore, she couldn't help it, every man willing to make a fool of himself. What nobody understands is how Sherm says he found her—drowned, then she came to, whispered, and died again."

"They think he did it?"

Baze shrugs, picks up a gilt-framed photo sitting on the table: a man with his wife and daughter. The women look the same except that the wife is resigned while the daughter, the set of her mouth and shoulders, belies panic, the wish to fly. Baze says, "Family heirloom?" I bought it at the flea market; it's no one I know. I say this. Baze says, "The only photograph in the place and it's of strangers. That's odd." I know what he means, odd like Garnett Shandy insisting I'm a good woman turned honky-tonk angel, not by God but an irresponsible, trifling husband.

"I like the idea of family," I tell Baze.

He asks if I have a radio. "That's how we'll get through this."

So we climb the narrow stairs. In bed, in the darkness, the radio providing a series of diverse, episodic rhythms to rock to, crackle and intrusive talk, we make love. Baze feels ordinary, small, a little soft. (The drinking all day, he explains.) It's over like that. (We've warmed to this for months, he says, I'm sorry, six months I've lived with the promise of you, I'm human.) There's no climax for me, just tears which I have so often with love they're no surprise, not even to Baze who runs his hand down my back, across my legs, more; I feel the callouses, pleasure rising to my throat. He says, touching my face, Don't worry, it means you have a Soul. For that minute love feels lush, like rain falling.

I slide into sleep and dream I walk on icy streets. It's Sunday morning and I have good clothes on: Am I going somewhere? Coming home? I dream I'm awake then and crossing the hall to my bathroom, a small room, a pantry converted years ago, Garnett calls it the water closet, painted a startling, heady blue by some previous tenant: the color a falling star makes streaking towards a frozen river. Baze is there, I've interrupted him. As I see him naked for the first time in light, I realize why he's been careful about clothes, what he hides, his *genitalia* a root which, as I appear, unfolds, grows like a vine, fills the room, latticing over walls, windows, the door. (You've never had it like this, he says.)

I wake in my own bed, empty.

Baze has gone.

The sun rises in the east, red and hot as if it were falling. I put on my white linen nightgown. That's what bedclothes are good for in the summer here, wandering around in in daylight hours, staying cool. I go onto my upstairs porch and lean over the rails. On the ridge of the highway I see a truck coming, Don and Garnett's. He'll drop her at the laundromat, then head to the gravel pit. She sits in the middle, next to him, never on the passenger side. As they move towards town, disappearing again, I remember what she once said: being careful, always making sure he knows I feel love, urges for it. I said, Is it enough? She said: Yes, yes.

In the field across the way a tractor begins its spiral. The uncut wheat in the center is silver. The wind undulates its surface, runs it like the tide must run the ocean. The mowed wheat in the trail behind the thrasher is orange, prickly. I remember how the man in the one Hemingway book described his lover as having hair the color of cut wheat and wonder why, when he had the choice to see it as shimmering and phosphorescent, or as ruddy, the color of the verge of decay, he chose that. I'm obsequious about grim details too. I remember Baze, the smell of him, the thrust, the surprise I examine now, turn over in my hands like a clue. His wife's face, older than mine, not so pretty, appears in the periphery like my conscience. I push it away and think, instead, of driving one of those big thrasher-pulling tractors and writing my name and Baze's in the wheat with a heart and arrow, one of us loves the other. When I realize, though, that I don't know his last name I think instead, across the valley, visible from the air and everywhere, only my name, my signature: Eve.

The Joe Lewis Story

When I was nineteen years old and newly moved to the city from my hometown Siren and living in the apartment above the diner I worked at, and buying clothes and my home furnishings at Christian thrift stores and eating at work because that was what I could afford, my mind was free. And I spent time thinking about the year I was eighteen, the worst so far, a prism, black, like onyx: reflecting gray into the years since (only one then, I realize) but, worse, all the clean ones that came before.

At home, no one spoke, my sister Tina, pale and scared since the wreck; her reconstructed husband, Kent, silent, propped forward like a wire and cardboard statue. My brother Henry stared at the floor or wall and hardly took a bath or changed out of his filling station clothes. My father stayed in the basement with his reclining chair and whiskey. And when I had to visit them I went walking: past my school, past my father's store which my mother ran now, past the Foxtail Nightclub, the Bijou, the Dinner Bell, the Sporting Man's Bar. Memorials, all of them, to a Joe Lewis who was no boxer but my lover. The courtship began, middled, ended: spring unfolding, summer ripening. And the fall.

Clear vision arrives like that. I was driving my Pontiac one night, rain pouring, tree branches shaking at the sky, my windshield wipers malfunctioning, and though it was months later I realized in a flash that the tough-looking woman with red hair was one of the reasons Joe left town. She was gone, and since the day he was too. I said, as if to Joe, though he'd departed: Hard, Cruel, Loose. I should have seen it by the serpents in his tattoos.

She was what I wasn't. If he tried his tricks on her she'd do the dead man's float, away, away.

Foresight is often mistaken for no courage. Joe said as we lay on the mattress on the floor one cold night, "Live a little, Janie, gamble. Fly." I heard fry. Out of the firing pan and into the fry.

Anyway, I grew up slowly, playing with dolls and telling stories by the time most girls were French-kissing. In high school I wore thick glasses and talked about great books and my best friend was Anna, and my father called us Mutt and Jeff because she was short and I was clumsy. There's a picture of us under the apple tree in the back yard, blossoms puffing out over us, and we're wearing dresses we'd designed to make ourselves look better. The story begins like this:

There were flowers blooming, bugs humming. The air had that wet smell, and the grass was pale and thick. We should have been studying. We stood on the stairs outside school and Anna said, "We should skip." I said, "We might get in trouble." She said, "I'd like to see how the other kids feel." So we stood behind a tree so no one would see us, and I said, "Now what?" Anna said, "We should go somewhere, like to Willie's apartment."

Anna's brother, Willie, had just come back from California with a woman named Claire, and they got married on the patio behind Anna's parents' house. Claire wore an antique dress, purple, a little ragged, beads hanging down, and sandals. Her oldest daughter, Syvette (eleven), was the maid of honor, and Fae (six) carried flowers. It was a time, 1975, when Willie went to California because college hemmed him in. I thought about what I'd read and heard and I pictured him there, working in a factory packing vegetables I'd never heard of, breathing air different from ours. But I missed him being at college. Anna and I used to take the bus to see him and his friend, Ted, and they'd take us to a museum or out for sandwiches. I loved them both and the words they used: *humanitarian, alienation, hunger, prescience, peace.*

Now Ted lived alone, and Willie lived here, in Siren, above the Sporting Man's with Claire and her children. Anna's dad bought the bar for Willie so he'd have a way to support his new family.

We went down the hill, down main street, past all of the businesses, still closed or just open. I remember the day, stepping along in shiny shoes, my peach dress with the creamy roses, Anna beside me in stripes to make her tall. We passed my father's Appliance and Used Furniture Store, closed, the Foxtail Nightclub, just opening, and came to the corner: the Sporting Man's Bar. We went in the back door and climbed a stairwell with swirling rails in the banister, the pool table and cigarette machine just below. Upstairs, in the apartment, Willie and Claire were lying down on a big cushion on the floor.

Willie said, "We bartend at night and the kids get home at three." Claire was wearing Chinese pajamas, with dragons. She tossed her hair out of her face and said, "Why are you girls dressed up?"

Anna said, "We made these dresses, Claire. We finished them last night at Janie's and, you know, to experiment, but also to relax, we poured whiskey in our glasses of Coke and Janie's mother caught us."

Claire smiled. "How?"

She'd ducked her head in the sewing room door and said, "How's the project, dears?" Then she frowned, sniffed, poured our drinks down the laundry room drain, and said, "You see, I noticed only one empty can of Coke in the garbage pail, and I knew one can didn't make two drinks this tall." And she worried we felt sad or guilty, or she felt sad and guilty, and in the morning, to be cheerful, she came to my bedroom with Henry's trumpet and played. We clapped. Then she cooked breakfast and took pictures of us in our new dresses before we left for school.

Anna said, "She didn't get mad."

Claire said, "That's sweet."

Willie said, "Ted's coming for the summer, to work in the bar."

Anna loved Ted. "I'm so glad," she said.

I was staring at a framed photo on top of the TV, and I crossed the room to pick it up. "Who is this?" I asked. He was wearing jeans and a black leather vest, open, nothing underneath it.

Willie said, "Joe Lewis."

The name seemed familiar. "Is he famous?" I asked.

Claire said, "His feet stink, he treats women like shit, he's wanted in Indiana, he wears pants with a hole in the crotch, and his balls hang out. He's famous for that." I looked again, at his eyes, pale blue, his naked chest and shoulders.

The mountains behind him seemed small.

Willie said, "Claire hates him. I don't know why."

"I like that vase," I said, pointing.

Claire said, "It's a bong." She filled it, handed it to me.

"Good stuff," Anna said, sucking hard, her lips pursed. I coughed and Willie pounded my back. Then sound disappeared and I heard it missing: a white, high-pitched roar. "The walls come together now," Claire said. That's what I thought she said. It seemed odd, but that's what Anna remembers Claire saying too. Also: "Welcome, welcome."

A night soon after that, at home, we were eating dinner. We saved the dining room for guests, four layers over the table: a pad, cloth, lace overlay, plastic to protect the lace. On regular nights we ate at the drop-leaf in the kitchen. On this particular night, we had potatoes, sirloin steak, salad with vinegar dressing, my father's favorite meal. He said, "Henry, scrape your teeth against your fork one more time and I'll wipe the wall with you."

The telephone rang. My mother answered it. "Tina," she said, pacing back and forth in her pullover and slacks, and matching shoes. "Life is like that." She twisted the phone cord. "Yes, it is," she said. She hung up. My father said, "After a hard day's work a man needs a few drinks and it's time Tina learned that."

My mother said, "Well, I know. But she dropped a piece of flatware down the drain and it got mangled in the garbage disposal, and that depressed her. And she sits there, no one to talk to, dinner on the table, no idea where Kent is, and the sun goes down and the house gets chilly. You should feel that way just once."

My father said, "My problems are worse." He yanked on the book I was reading and said, "Pretty soon, Janie, damn it, you're going to be looking for work and you won't have anything to write on your application except that you read." I did read: hard books for school, paperbacks, all the magazines that came to the house, books my mother got in the mail and, at night and on weekends, all my old favorites. I was reading *Heidi*.

My father tucked his napkin into his shirt collar, picked up his knife and fork. "If I had to say any of my kids were smart," he said, "I'd say Henry."

Henry looked up, calm-looking. He isn't calm.

My mother rocked her chair back and forth. "I used to feel that way about music," she said, "the way Janie feels about books." She was remembering life before she met Father. She was twenty-seven, giving piano lessons in frothy-sleeved dresses; he was twenty-four, in the Army, stationed in Georgia. She hummed something, then tipped her chair back down. "I want to go home," she said, "before everyone I know gets old and dies."

My father said, "Henry and I are planning a fishing trip."

Henry said, "What?"

I said, "Henry should go to college."

Mother said, "School makes him nervous."

My father said, "The gas station is the right kind of work for Henry."

Henry didn't answer. I wondered if he was remembering first grade, the day he left when the teacher said it was recess because he thought school was over and he was supposed to come home. My father took him to the basement and hit him with the razor strap. I was in my bedroom, standing over the floor register, holding my doll and sucking my thumb. Henry didn't cry until it was over. My father left. "Honey, hush," my mother said. She was in the basement too. Henry knew what recess was after that but he kept coming home anyway, every day.

I was in the park, a triangle of grass next to the hospital, the hospital a pink one-story brick building. I used to think every town was exactly like Siren. I don't now. Anyway, I was waiting for Anna, reading *The Secret Garden* and, for the first time, sick of it: white-faced Colin locked in a room and yellow-faced Mary and the healthy boy and good food that cured them, and the ending, Colin wobbling across blooms saying, Father, Father. I shut the book and used it for a pillow and lay there in the sun, waiting. Anna threw her jacket onto the ground and shook her hair and it flared, wild. She said, "Ted gets here Friday. This will be the summer he decides he loves me. I feel it."

I said, "What's an orgasm?" I'd seen the word in a magazine article called "Secrets Women Keep," and I was confused about the details.

Anna said, "You thrash and shriek and relax afterwards. It happens to all men and some women who are good in bed." She leaned close and said, "There's something I want to say. When Willie and Claire bartended once, I baby-sat for Syvette and Fae, and they were asleep and Ted showed up, and I was standing at the window, looking out at the flashing lights of the little businesses, the cars puttering past on main street, and I looked toward the city limits, the highway, the trucks roaring by, and I wondered when my life would change. And Ted touched me . . ." She put her hand on my face and it trickled down my neck like water. "And kissed me."

My skin prickled. Who would kiss me, I wondered, when?

"I made that up," Anna said.

I was picturing Willie and Claire's apartment, the tall windows and vaulted ceiling, the soft cushion on the floor to lie on. I was remembering a dream, a man's touch, his words, the awakening. "That's the way it should be," I said. We left the park then. Anna said, "When Ted gets here let's go to the bar and have drinks. Friday." She was talking about June 24, 1975, the night Joe Lewis came to Siren and for a while after the highway seemed like a tidal river, a place swift and salty where trouble didn't grow.

JUNE 24, 1975

My father laid the newspaper down and yanked on his necktie, green with orange flecks. "Energy crisis my ass," he said, "someone made that up."

I was reading a book I'd bought at a yard sale: a man wandering across the world because his wife died in a wreck and he'll never be happy but he meets a girl in the rain at a cemetery, whose father was murdered, and he avenges the death. *The Sunlit Ambush*.

"You should study stenography" my father said.

I said, "Most people don't use stenography now. They have dictaphones."

He said, "Don't be smart."

The telephone rang. My mother answered it.

I said to Henry, "Did you have a good day?"

He cleared his throat. "I took the pollution-control shit off someone's car," he said, "so they don't have to buy unleaded."

My mother said, "Janie, telephone. It's Anna."

I sat on the stairs and held the receiver between my neck and shoulder and cracked my knuckles. Anna said, "I called to tell you what I'm wearing. Don't overdress. We'll seem immature."

My father said, "Get back to the table before I get mad."

I said, "A fat pig with a mouth so huge and rotten that when he talks it's like being on the edge of the landfill, staring in."

Anna said, "Who? What?"

I saw my father's fist, raised. "Right, Anna," I said. I kept talking. "That's right, Anna." It was the first time he'd tried; it was the first time I'd been impolite. I ducked. The light-switch plate behind my head cracked and fell to the floor.

He said, "You'll pay for that and you can't leave the house for two weeks."

He sent me to my room, but I climbed out the window onto the porch roof and down the tree with the tree house in it. Henry watched from his room. My mother hung out the window above me, her hair sliding out of the bobby pins and onto her shoulders.

"Janie, please," she said, "I'll sleep in your room tonight and I won't let him hit you."

I'd heard her say that before but not to me.

And I was about to go in the back door of the Sporting Man's Bar and upstairs to Willie and Claire's apartment, and Henry came around the corner and out of the alley, hell-bent. He grabbed me. "You should go to college," he said. I said I didn't know how you got in. I said, "It's expensive, I think." He said, "Well, go somewhere. I have a little money if you need it." He crossed the street and went to the Foxtail Nightclub to drink.

Upstairs, Willie and Claire were getting ready for work. "One last hit," Claire said. She lit the bong. Fae stood on her head. Syvette was lying on the cushion on the floor in the center of the room, wriggling her hips. "Cha cha cha," she said. "When I grow up I want to be one of those women who pose in magazines."

Claire said, "As soon as the girls go to sleep, Janie, come downstairs and have a drink."

I said, "Where's Anna?"

Willie and Claire left.

Anna said, "Here I am." She walked in the room with Ted. She said, "See what he gave me." It was a wall hanging made of twigs and seashells.

Ted said, "I've got something for you too, Janie. I bought you both something for graduation." Anna was disappointed, I know. Ted gave me a pair of earrings made with beads and wire and chips of bone. I put them in. "Thank you," I said.

He said, "Now, let's all three go the bar."

I'd put six quarters in the jukebox.

I was drinking my first beer ever. I'd eaten a pickled, hard-boiled egg and a bag of peanuts, and was thinking about trying cigarettes, when the swinging doors in the corner opened and a man walked in and said, "Would you believe me if I said I was the floor show?" He looked like a cowboy but not quite. His eyes shone like live coals. He said, "I'm trying to find my friend Willie Sanders." I waved but Willie couldn't see me. "Willie," I said, "the man from the picture on your TV is here."

Willie ran around the end of the bar.

"My man," Joe said. They slapped hands in the air. They pounded each other's backs. Claire watched, eyes narrow. She said: "Do they have a warrant for your arrest in California now?"

Joe said, "No. Thank you for your concern."

Willie asked Claire to stay at the Sporting Man's and tend bar, and the rest of us went across the street to the Foxtail Nightclub.

I looked around for Henry.

Anna said, "This is like old times except Joe's here now."

Willie said, "What haven't you told me, Joe? Why does Claire hate you?"

He shrugged.

Ted said, "She's a fine woman."

Willie said, "Let's buy these girls some fancy drinks."

It was my first time inside the Foxtail. The upholstery was leopard-skin plastic, and an Englebert Humperdinck song was playing. I was having an ice cream cocktail in a stemmed glass with floating nuts, and a short man with a red nose walked up and said, "Excuse me, but I'm doing a survey. What's your bra size?"

Joe threw a bar stool over. He said, "Is this how men talk to women around here?"

Ted said, "Actually, yes."

Willie said, "Take it easy, Joe."

People backed off like they do in movies. The man said, "I didn't mean any harm."

I saw Henry on the outskirts. Tina's husband, Kent, walked up and said, "What's the trouble, buddy?" He put his arm around the short guy. "Get him out of here," Joe said, "or I'll kill him."

Later, I asked, "Would you really?"

Willie and Claire were closing the Sporting Man's.

Anna and Ted were looking after Syvette and Fae. I was walking down the street with Joe Lewis, and we stopped in front of the Bijou to look at a movie poster of a caged bear heading into the wilderness on a train. I said, "Are you really wanted in Indiana?"

He said, "Not for anything glamorous."

I tipped my head back and looked at the streetlights, the familiar outlines of buildings. Siren seemed like the inside of my house, cramped. Joe said, "Did you have a good childhood? Was there enough money? Did it feel safe?" His questions seemed strange, but I found out later his mother had hung herself when he was seven. He touched the lapel of my jacket. One of my earrings caught on his sleeve and I pulled away and heard the plink-plinking of beads and pieces of bone as they dropped to the sidewalk. I put my finger on his lips, which seemed soft and pink, no softer or pinker than anyone's, I suppose; but there they were in the middle of that stern face, that black and wiry beard.

"Janie," he said, "please."

There was no place to go. He laid his jacket down like a blanket in a field of weeds and took his clothes off and kneeled above me. I searched his face, and nothing happened. I thought about what Anna had said and, when he pushed himself in, shut my eyes and screamed. He stood up. His penis arched away from his body like a hook, wet and glistening in the moonlight. I said, "What exactly is an orgasm then?" He lay down again and showed me. It was nothing like I expected: power, calamity, voltage. It was related to pain. Afterwards, he wrapped me in his coat. I pointed across the field and said, "That's where I live." He said, "Who's that?" Under the porch light my mother paced back and forth in her orange bathrobe, carrying a flashlight, pointing its tiny beam into the hills and trees and shadows.

JULY

Joe was working third shift at the boat factory and living above a garage. I was wearing a green dress I'd made myself, and heels, carrying a stenographer's notebook. I knocked on his door. He answered in cutoffs, barefoot. Pieces of fiberglass always stuck to his clothes, his socks especially, and gave him rashes. "Queenie," he said, "did you get the job?"

I said, "They said they want someone who's married and settled down."

He said, "Let's go for a walk."

We went down the railroad tracks. I tottered from tie to tie. I said, "What went wrong in Indiana?" I'd pictured robbery, a gun-fight, smashed windows, scrawled angry words on the city hall walls, a down-spiral of right action and Joe Lewis, misunderstood. He said, "I owe child support." My choices seemed narrow then: hate or love, good or evil. Claire: "He's a vile, irresponsible man." Willie: "He's a nice guy who had tough breaks."

Joe said, "My life is rootless." He picked up a stone and threw it. "You look fresh as summer night in that dress, Janie. If I left Siren now it would be to make things good for my daughter."

We walked back to town and down the alley so we wouldn't pass in front of the plate-glass windows of my father's store. I couldn't imagine his reaction to Joe (Joe's clothes, Joe's words, Joe's age, the fact that Joe wore dark glasses even when there wasn't sun). We passed the back door, the stacked-up empty appliance boxes, the dumpster. Joe said, "Will you inherit this?" I'd never thought of it. "One way or another," I said.

We went back to his apartment, and I lay on the floor while

he sat in his recliner with the stuffing popping out and read the dictionary. He always did. I asked him why once. He said, "To increase my word power and influence people." A chilly breeze wafted the palm-frond curtains hanging in the windows.

I yawned and stared at the ceiling.

Joe said, "A girl like you could save a recalcitrant bastard like me."

I used his dictionary to look the word up: stubborn, defiant. "Like Heidi's grandfather," I said. Joe hadn't read it. I said, "He drank and gambled and left his son to be raised by strangers, and the son got married and had a baby, but the son died and so did his wife and the grandfather had to raise Heidi himself, and she made him good and glad to be alive."

Joe said, "The girl in the mountains who goes around with goats?"

I said, "Yes."

He said, "It sounds perverted."

AUGUST

"Daddy and I aren't getting along," my mother said. She tucked herself into the bed next to mine—it used to be Tina's, twin beds. She said, "I know you have a boyfriend now because someone told me and I won't tell your father but please spend time with Tina because she's lonesome."

I went to Tina's for the afternoon and she set a quart of gin on the counter.

"I like it in juice," she said. She showed me the afghan she was making, the calendar, the hook rug: WELCOME. "How about these for Christmas?" she said. She showed me a picture of stuffed letters that spelled NOEL, TIDINGS, CHEER. She sat across from me on the couch and drank. "You must be excited," she said, "your first lover. I remember the night I let Kent." Her knees flapped open and shut. "I let him," she said, "and it was over."

SEPTEMBER

My father and Henry came back from their fishing trip and stood in the driveway next to the truck. My father said to my mother: "I've brought you pins that look like falling leaves, malachite-and-silver rings. I want us to be happy, no fights again, ever. I can't imagine, though, who put gravel in my gas tank."

Henry was cleaning the cab of the truck: cellophane wrappers from candy, beer cans, foil packets of ketchup and mustard, beer cans, styrofoam cartons, slips of paper, beer cans.

"Did you have a good time?" I asked.

He put the garbage in a bag, put it in the trash, and put the lid on.

My father said, "Imagine the warped mind of the person who'd put gravel in my gas tank."

I said, "Did you have a good time, Henry?" He smiled.

OCTOBER

Every weekend we drove two hundred miles away to visit the airport because Joe liked the idea. "Planes landing," he said, "planes taking off, suitcases climbing the ramp into the belly of the plane, planes spitting the suitcases back out." As for me, I remember I stood in the ladies' bathroom and dried my hands with the blow machine and wondered what I'd ever be.

I couldn't think of anything, except a mother, maybe, and I envisioned a dark-haired baby girl, her ears pierced with rubies, me pushing the collapsible stroller down the airport promenade, a scarf wrapped around my head as if I were a gypsy, and Joe Lewis beside me in roving clothes, but his face stern and serious after all, concerned for the future. I thought: my mother was married in a brown suit, and Tina, the November before last, in expensive white. I cried. I stood there. The hot air blew into my hands and the water evaporated. "Joe Lewis," I said, "marry me, please."

NOVEMBER

It was a bleak day with slate-colored trees webbed against the sky. I was lying on my back on the mattress on the floor in Joe's cold room. In the kitchen, on the sill between the pane of glass and windowscreen, Joe kept cold cuts, mustard, mayonnaise, butter, a loaf of bread on a chair nearby. He couldn't afford a refrigerator. I was thinking about that and how, the way things went, he'd never get one or a table or a couch either, also that he was coming to my house that night for dinner to meet my father (my mother's idea). He was on his knees, pointing at himself, a supplication. "Put your mouth on it," he said, "Janie, please."

"I don't see what it has to with sex," I said, finally.

He put his shirt on, his socks, his pants. He said, "Virgins are overrated." He said other things too. We put warm coats on and walked down the highway to the boat factory so Joe could get his check. The lake wasn't frozen yet. The waves chopped up, sharp. Joe threw flat stones. He left me waiting in the parking lot for an hour. I stood outside the corrugated, slant-roof building and people walked past and waved.

Joe came back and said, "I forgot about you, Queenie. I was playing cards."

I stomped my feet to make the blood roll. I cried.

Joe said, "Come on, I'll buy you breakfast at the Dinner Bell."

At the Dinner Bell I saw Delbert, my father's friend he snowmobiled with, also my twelfth-grade teacher and the Methodist minister. I pretended I was no one, not Janie at least; I wondered, sitting there as though I'd just arrived in Siren, my past a blank to fill in, who could I be? Was my life good or bad?

I drank cocoa and Joe read the Duluth paper, and I asked for the funnies but they were on the back of the sports page and he said no. The waitress walked up, a thin girl with a small, square mouth. Her hair rolled away from its center part like cotton batting on a spool, dyed red. She said, "If it isn't Joe Lewis." She set the plates down and I saw a tattoo between her ring and middle finger: a black spider on a blue web.

Joe said, "Thank you."

She walked away and I said, "She isn't from here."

Joe said, "That's what I like about her."

We had a fight that afternoon because I asked Joe to wash his hair and change out of his fiberglass-speckled clothes before he met my father. He did, finally; even so, when the back door to the house opened and Joe walked in, my father stood up from the kitchen table, threw his newspaper down, and, shock registering in the slackness of his face, said, "Where's your home, son?"

Joe said, "Just about anywhere."

They shook hands for a long time, and eyed each other. My mother said, "I hope you like meat loaf."

Henry asked him what he drove and Joe showed us pictures of his Harley-Davidson and told us how he'd had it for eleven years, as he'd lived in four states and two dozen different apartments or houses. That's when my father went to the basement to sit in his chair and drink, which he'd done before, but this was the first time I ever remember that he spent a night there.

Most importantly, the phone rang, shrill.

Joe had gone home.

Henry was in his room.

My mother and I were washing dishes.

She answered it, squeezed her eyes shut and said, "Oh no, please. No. Yes. Yes. Thank you."

When she hung up, she bumped the desk and the pencils in the jar fell, clacking, to the floor.

I picked them up. I said, "What's wrong?"

She said, "Tina and Kent have been in a wreck. Tonight is crucial."

For no reason I fathomed I thought of the sign they put on the city pond in winter, THIN ICE, and the black water below. We drove to the hospital. In the pink lobby, we kept a vigil. "I pray that I have thanks to give, Lord in heaven in the name of Jesus Thy Son," my mother said. It was the first time she'd used religion since my father's adultery, a long time ago. A nurse hovered nearby. I called Joe: no answer. I concentrated on a crack that wandered like lightning through the brick wall. The only other person was Kent's friend, the short man with the red nose who'd asked me, in June, what my bra size was, and Joe Lewis rushed in like a fool or angel; no other man I'd ever met would. The short man sat across from us and held a bottle of schnapps. He said, "They should put together a convoy of ambulances and take this problem to a city big enough to fix it."

DECEMBER

On Christmas Eve I put my coat on, my scarf and gloves and cap, and walked to the Sporting Man's. I opened the door and smoky air hit my face. I felt the heat, the familiar blood-stinging pleasure, respite after trauma. I was cold, getting warmer. Willie stood behind the bar. He said, "I can't believe you're walking around in weather like this, Janie. Drink some bourbon."

I sat at a table with Anna and Claire and Ted. Joe was on the other side of the bar, shooting pool with the waitress from the Dinner Bell. Anna said, "College isn't hard. You do what you're told, and people say afterwards that you're smart. I got A's, A A A and A."

Joe was wearing tight pants, a black shirt with swirly designs and snaps, a red necktie with green trees: Christmas gear. He walked up to our table, thumped his pool cue, and said, "Sleighbells ring, children glisten." He wiggled his hips. "Cha cha cha," he said. Also, "Hello, Queenie, good-bye."

He went back to the pool table to shoot. Claire went upstairs to the apartment.

Ted stared after her. "Her hair is the most beautiful color," he said.

Anna said, "It's brown." Hers was black.

Joe sat down.

Ted said, "I'll never find a woman like that for myself."

Joe said, "Count your blessings."

Ted frowned, then followed Claire.

Joe said, "It makes her feel young." He left to shoot pool.

I looked at the ice cubes in my glass.

When Joe came back, he said, "Claire needs a soft place to lie down now but that doesn't stop her from risking it for old time's sake, and in front of anyone who cares to watch, poor Willie."

The red-haired waitress was getting ready to shoot.

She twisted her face, frowned down the cue, pulled her arm back . . .

Anna said, "I learned in a class that, for some people, sex is like pushing the panic button. The Escape Button. Release."

Joe said, "Pardon me."

Anna pointed at the red-haired waitress. "Take her, for instance. She lived with a man and left him for his brother and left him for a man she moved here with, and she married his boss, then split up with him. And each time she had a kid and left it too."

Joe waved the waitress over to our table. He said, "Have you been in love with ten men in ten years?" She didn't answer. She was wearing a T-shirt, nothing underneath it, a skull and crossbones on the front: CAUTION, it said, CONTENTS MAY BE HARMFUL.

He said, "Have you had ten children?"

She said, "Something like that." She reached down and sipped his drink. "Every spring I go into heat, get myself serviced, and drop a litter."

He said, "I think that's marvelous."

Anna said, "I'm going upstairs."

It was the three of us then: Joe, the waitress, me.

The waitress sat down.

She said, "What I love about you, Joe, is your name. It reminds me of a story I heard when I was a little girl, about a man who was going to die in the electric chair and he sat there, arms strapped down, the wires about to quiver, death in his face. What do you think he said?" She reached in Joe's pocket for a cigarette and lit it. She said, " 'Joe Louis, save me please.' Isn't that lovely?"

I said, "It's spelled different." I knew that at least, who the other Joe Lewis (Louis) was.

She shrugged.

Anna came downstairs.

She said, "Ted. The flashing lights, the window, his profile in it. You remember, Janie? But it's Claire with him, not me."

"I'm going home," I said.

I reminded Joe about Christmas dinner at my house. I said, "Don't worry about my father because he'll probably stay in the basement." He came upstairs only for work now, and he was working less all the time and my mother was working more.

I said good-bye to Willie and that was the last time I saw him. Anna was sad and I wanted to help but couldn't. Snow crunched under my boots as I walked towards home and, for the last time, felt hard and sunk about my family, Tina especially, the startled look on her face, the bandages wound around her head, crutches beside her, the sprawl of her as she sat next to Kent (stitched, plastered, splinted, his mouth wired shut; he smiled and his face contorted). The doctors said Tina needed practice. She drew pictures and worked on the alphabet. "Janie," she said, "Janie-brainy, Janie-doodle," things like that.

It was a sleepless night or if I had sleep I confused it with waking, my dreams with life. I was in a small room, draperies hanging down, my mother out of sight but speaking. She said, "Can I save you? Are you doing things you shouldn't? I've never had an orgasm." (Was I dead, I wondered, or pretending not to hear?) She said, "You're going far away. Come back. I'll run your life." When I woke she was sitting on the end of my bed. "Get up," she said, "it's Christmas day."

Downstairs, Henry was turning the pages of a magazine. Tina sat next to Kent, who sat in his wheelchair, silver-and-gold and red-and-green colored gifts in his lap. I thought about my father in the basement and asked my mother how he was. She said, "He has a TV and whiskey down there. He comes up for food in the middle of the night. Don't dwell on it." She played the piano: O PROMISE ME YOUR LOVE WILL SOMEDAY MEET ME IN THE SKY. When she finished she asked me, "Is your boyfriend coming for dinner?"

I called Joe: no answer.

Henry was pacing the floor. He said, "I look at this mess every day."

I dialed Willie and Claire's number.

Claire answered.

I said, "Is Joe there?"

She paused. "Didn't he tell you?"

Only in the drama of hindsight, I suppose, was I shoving premonition into place, symbols toward their upshot. In memory, I was sick; in truth, just curious. What had Joe done? Had he thrown away or carried with him to the next town his hope for a force or vision, a girl or woman, who'd save a recalcitrant bastard like that? Was he bored? Or desperate? And what about me? In the act of salvage, would I solidify, or dissolve?

"He left," Claire said.

I pictured a street, a sidewalk, a white house with a fence, a sweet-faced baby with dark eyes and pearly teeth; I remembered Joe, the starlit night, his sigh, these words: "If I left Siren now it would be to make things right for my daughter."

Henry was pacing the floor behind me. "Of all the things I miss," he said, "I miss my mind."

"Indiana," I told Claire.

There was silence on the line.

In the background, I heard fretting, shrieks, complaints, the children. "Yvette, stop that," Claire said, "Fae, go away."

"Joe went to Indiana to make a good life for his daughter," I told Claire.

The clamor behind her increased and ended.

"No," she said, "he didn't."

Years have passed since but only in the single one after did I dream that my breathing stopped: in the gray morning, as city traffic swelled outside the window of my apartment above the diner, as I lay in my narrow bed and passed, it seemed, across the horizon between void and grace, rock and water, between a state of sand and a solution too deep and fast and endless, I opened my mouth for air and something fell in. What was it?

I spat it out: a scrap of paper.

Tina recovered and left Kent and took up short dresses and several men at once, lighting in the end on one who was the same as Kent and worse. Kent drives a truck in California. My mother keeps a chair in the basement next to my father's—a Lazy Boy for Girls—but she doesn't use it. "He needs his privacy," she says. I see Henry the most of all; he carries a gun in his glovebox and he gave me one too, for under my bed, and a club he designed himself—studded with nails, lethal. He said, "If not this gun or club, Janie, a brick or knife will do."

I took the bus to the airport one day to meet Anna as she passed through the city. "Willie and Claire split up," she said. "Claire lives above the Bijou with a nineteen-year-old man and Willie has a girlfriend who keeps the vacuum cleaner plugged in all the time because she uses it five or six times a day. Fae lives with Claire. Syvette is sixteen, grown up, with a baby and a place of her own."

She leaned forward. "Do you hear from Joe Lewis?" she asked.

He called once and asked me to send him money. He said, "I remember the feel of you in my arms, your agitated heart . . ." I hung up. "No," I said, "never." The story ends like this:

On a day of the week I didn't work, I was wearing a hat with feathers, a coat with fur, beads on my dress; I'd bought it all at a thrift store the day before. I was downtown, having returned a library book, *Amore,* and I stopped at a delicatessen to buy a hard-boiled egg. As the handsome man in the white hat seasoned it for me with peppers and cream, I considered what the book had said: that people broke up, down, apart, because of it, that one lover was always stronger and, once the disclosure was made, once the cat escaped the bag and someone sang, love turned demolition and the other lover ended in a corner. The man gave me my egg. I left. I waded through traffic and pictured my apartment where, dirt banished, every rug in its place, the chime and buzz of the diner below, I wanted to stay, under the wing of the eaves, lulled, beyond trouble.

Enough

I walk into the bar I work at, which is called Home. The idea is that when people want to know where you've been or where you're going, you say Home. At first friends used to ask, "Are you safe? Couldn't a nice-looking girl like you get a better job?" Customers still say, "You? The bartender? You must be tougher than you look." I flip the TV channel, pour beer, set a stein down hard.

"Hey! You can't just walk in here and change channels," Marvin, who drinks warm Budweiser, says.

"I just did."

I don't smile.

I have tuned the Playboy Channel out and a station that shows country-and-western videos in. I hate the Playboy Channel, naked women spinning like pinwheels on the screen above me. George Strait is on the screen now, mournfully handsome, wearing a white hat, singing "I lost my wife and a girlfriend, somewhere along the way."

"Give me a break," Marvin says.

"Where would you like it?"

"You need new material," he says.

I nod. I look at myself in the mirror above the cash register. I didn't fix my eyes today. My hair is slung back in a ponytail. Bill, my favorite customer, leans over and touches my hand. One of his spurs clanks on the base of his barstool. "Are you all right?" he asks.

"I didn't have time to put my face on," I say.

"I see that. Plainer than usual," he says, "but still mighty easy on the eyes."

I hear rumors Bill wears his hat to bed. "You're simple to impress," I say.

"It's your no-good boyfriend," he says.

I shake my head.

"Acting up," he says.

"No."

Once, when my boyfriend was acting up, I got drunk and told Bill. In his pickup, parked by the river, I said, "Bill, kiss me, touch me." I wanted his hands on me all over. He took his hat off. "I'd love to," he said, "but you seem gun-shy." He didn't look like Bill then, his bald head shiny as the moon, but like a beast from a fable, a friendly one to lead the lost child home.

The barroom door opens and Don walks in. Edna, who is his wife, though they don't live in the same house anymore, says, "You were supposed to meet me here at five o'clock." She taps her watch. "It's eight o'clock now."

Don says, "And you stayed here and drank your dinner."

"I had to visit with my favorite bartender, Roxanne," Edna says, pointing at me. She's a wiry woman, forty-eight years old, and she dyes her hair a wicked shade of copper. Once she rode in a car with Ferlin Husky while he wrote a song. "Come here and give me a kiss, honey." I think she's talking to Don but she means me. She leans across the bar and kisses me.

Dixie sits down next to Edna and says, "Have they been in here yet?"

I wipe the bar down. "No," I say, "but quit chasing them." We're discussing Dixie's husband and the secretary at the feed mill where he works. They don't hide their affair. Dixie joins them at their table and buys the secretary beers.

Edna says, "I've heard of bending over backwards, Dixie, but you lay right down."

Dixie says, "I just don't want anyone to say I've been harsh." She slides her large, soft body up to the bar and below her black, piled-up hair, her earrings shine. She says, "All those years Dwayne came home late, and I served him his dinner on a TV tray in the living room, and I never sassed him."

"You should start," Edna says.

Dixie says, "I never went to a bar until I heard he was stepping out. I need a drink. My hands are shaking."

The marriage counselor my ex-husband, Darrell, and I used to see told me to quit throwing things at Darrell, who is a big man, because it scared him. I said, "He scares me when he doesn't come home until dawn and lurches into walls and knocks pictures down, and falls over with his underwear around his ankles." The marriage counselor said, "Perhaps. But perhaps he drinks to escape you." For months I didn't hold a stool against Darrell's chest to pin him down when I yelled, or smash glass against the wall. He appreciated it, he said. He came home on time and stopped carrying a fifth in his glovebox. He said he thought how good his life had become and it was because I'd stood beside him. He said this in the grocery store parking lot, his head tipped back to enjoy the sun. And he got drunk for two weeks. I threw a power drill when he came home. I threw it at the wall, not Darrell.

Edna says, "What you need is a man who treats you good, but not so good you get bored."

A man who was courting me a long time ago said that. He sold vacuum cleaners on a route between here and Tupelo; it turned out he had a girl in Tupelo.

Edna says, "Don keeps me on my toes."

Toes have never been important to me.

Other parts are. I met Darrell at a club where I danced on a platform in a fringed outfit, wearing a cowboy hat and waving toy pistols. He bought me a drink. I told him I was going to quit dancing because my torso ached. "Your torso should be in the Louvre," he said, "which is a museum." My knees buckled. He fell to his that night in my living room when I appeared before him in a slip that was tight across the hips and see-through lace on top. "You look like a bride," he said. I told him I was going to apply to vocational school in Ponca City. He said, "You won't need me then." And he kicked a lamp over. I said, "That's an antique." He said, "I only broke the shade." I said, "The shade's an antique too." It had been my Aunt Cora's lamp. She also used to dance in clubs. Darrell threw it against the wall and unzipped his pants. "Let's get married," he said. His dick was straight and thick, indefatigable.

"Why did you show up in your coveralls?" Edna says to Don. "You were supposed to meet me here in your glad rags. We're going dancing."

Don picks up his car keys. "I'll be back in a little bit," he tells Edna. To me, he says, "Roxanne, don't let Edna keep drinking."

"Roxanne, are you seeing a boy now?" Dixie asks me.

"She is," Edna says. "That no-good who thinks he's too good to come in here."

My boyfriend Max doesn't come in the bar because he says it reminds him of bars in his one-horse hometown he had no choice but to frequent. "You should feel comfortable," I say. "I never liked them then," he says. "Please come for a while," I said on my birthday, when the owners bought a keg. "You work there," he said, "you have to go. I'll never go." His bar has orange fishnets on the ceiling and the jukebox plays rock-n-roll.

Edna says, "Don drinks with me and I think that's important."

Dixie says, "If you can't share your social life, what can you share?"

Max and I used to drink together in bed, a candle burning beside us. But lately he snorts speed until his mustache turns white and his dick stays soft. One morning, at dawn, after I'd tried for hours to raise him, he sat up, eyes shiny and red, hands clasped over his privates, and said, "I only care for you like a sister, Roxanne. You're an attractive woman, but not to me." The next day, he didn't remember. "How convenient," I said. He brought me flowers and fresh shrimp, which I don't like as well as the breaded kind. He stared at his hands. "What?" I said. He shook his head.

"Does he cheat?" Dixie asks.

Once, I went to his bar, Duke's, and there he was slumped in the corner with his arms around Betty Hondell, which is who he buys speed from. She turned around. "Hello, Betty," I said. "How is Tom-Joe and the baby?" She said, "Thank goodness it's only you, Roxanne." She pulled the straps of her dress back onto her shoulders. Max woke up. "Roxanne," he said, "my favorite girl." On the way home, in Betty's car, he slept with his head propped up against the infant seat, and Betty said, "I'm not looking to end my marriage." I said, "You wouldn't want him if you knew his secret." The next morning I made noise in the kitchen just to wake him. I said, "Do you feel attracted to Betty Hondell?" He said, "One lover doesn't seem like enough."

"I can stand chewing, gambling, smoking, and drinking," Edna says, "but not cheating."
"As for me," Dixie says, "my priority is to have a man say 'Did you have a good day, honey?' And if I didn't, run me a bath or rub my feet."

"Roxanne," Max said to me on the phone once, "did you have a good day?"
I said, "I had a miscarriage. Your baby or Darrell's I have no idea." It was true. I'd slept with both of them in the same month, the month Darrell left. Max said, "Pardon me?" I said, "I was driving. Snow was falling. The car fishtailed. I never made it to the

hospital." Max said, "Can I bring you something? Alka-Seltzer? Sanitary napkins?"

He brought chicken soup, a loaf of bread, a bag of tea from the health food store with a label that read: Herbs Used Since Ancient Days to Harmonize a Woman's Ways. He said, "I know you're depressed because you lost the baby." He fluffed a pillow on the couch and said, "But I would have paid for your abortion." I said, "My what?" He slid his hand inside my robe and snapped my sanitary belt. He said, "Let's get a place together."

Edna pulls a Kleenex out of her purse. "Oh, God," she says.

"Edna," I say. "What's wrong?"

"I hate Christmas carols." She leans over and lays her face on the bar.

I listen as I watch TV. I say, "Edna, that's Dolly Parton singing 'I Will Always Love You.'"

"It doesn't matter." She sobs. She crushes the Kleenex in her hand.

"Edna," I say, "it's February."

The door opens. "I'm back," Don says. He looks at Edna. "What's wrong with her?"

"Nothing I can explain," I say.

Edna brightens. "Let's go, Don. Let's take my car." She flops her hand around on the bar. "I can't find my keys."

Don sits down. "Check your purse."

"They're not there," she says.

"Your pockets?" I suggest.

"Someone took them," Edna says. "While I was in the bathroom, someone took them and is coming back tonight after the bar closes to steal my car. If someone steals my car, I can't get to work. If I can't get to work, I won't be able to pay my bills. If I can't pay my bills, I won't have a place to live. Oh, God." She lays her head down on the bar.

"We'll find them," I say.

Edna turns to Don. "You picked them up before you went home. They're in the pocket of your coveralls."

"They are not."

"So, Roxanne," Dixie says, "do you have plans for the future?"

Edna says, "You were drunk, Don, and you picked up my keys and took them home."

"I was not drunk," Don says. He slams his fist down.

"Hey!" Marvin yells from a booth. "Cool out."

Bill looks at me from the pool table. "Roxanne?" he says. "Are you all right?"

Edna says, "I'm going back if I have to walk."

"It's a mile and a half," I say. "It's cold."

"Let her go," Don says.

She swipes at him with her blue vinyl purse.

Dixie says, "It's true that if a man treats you good you can't love him."

The door slams.

Dixie says, "If you have heaven all the time, you can't recognize it's heaven."

"Jesus." Bill pushes his hat back and stares at me.

"Don't start acting like them," Max said about the bar patrons when I first took the job. "I mean, I think you're vulnerable, being newly divorced."

"People fight to make up," Dixie says.

Bill says, "Roxanne, are you all right?"

Darrell packed his clothes and tools the night he left. "It'll always be like this," he said. "We'll always disagree." I was frying Kielbasa and I threw the pan, hot water and sausage too, on the floor.

"Compromise is the key," Max says when I want to leave, late in the day, and I'm tired. "You're crazy about me in the morning," he says, to make me stay. I am glad to find him then, big and salty-smelling, good to kiss. He never said he loved me even though I cried. The time he came close stands out in my mind. At sunset, on the porch, he said, "This is the first time I've cared at all." I said, "You love me." He kissed me. He leaned over and blocked the sun.

The door opens. "Dwayne," Dixie says.
"Where's the secretary?" I ask.
"I don't question good fortune," Dixie says.
"I found Edna stomping across the bridge," Dwayne says.
Don says, "To hell with her."
Dixie says, "You can't rush a good fight."

"Why do you cry?" Max asked today.
Today is Valentine's Day, the anniversary of my wedding, the first since Darrell left. "You want me to do something I can't do," Max said. "I love you," I said, "and I would love anyone I spend this much time with." He looked away. "Do you love me?" I said. "I suppose," he mumbled. "Say it," I said. He looked away.

Edna opens the door. "I'm back."

"I don't need someone who needs other lovers," I said.
Max said, "Don't make yourself miserable, Roxanne." I said, "You make me miserable. I used to be friends with Betty Hondell until you decided you want to fuck her." Max said, "I don't fuck her. I want to but I don't. Isn't that the point?"

Dixie holds a bottle of perfume. "Dwayne bought me this for Valentine's Day."
"Sweet," I say.
"I bet you didn't know what day it was."
Two barstools away, Don stands with his arms around Edna. "I love you, Old Toothless," she says.
"Bill," I say, "will you watch the bar for me?"

He clears his throat. "There's something I want to ask you, Rox-anne, about that time we went for a drive." He looks at his boots. "How about a cup of coffee after work?"

I say, "Please watch the bar for me while I fix my face and hair."

"Take your time," Bill says. "You're good-looking when you try."

In the bathroom I take my ponytail down and brush my hair. I turn my sweatshirt inside-out so the paint splatters don't show, and I dig in my purse for lipstick.

"Roxanne, telephone!"

I open the door.

Behind the bar, Bill and Marvin stand on chairs, hanging a spray-painted bedsheet that reads: Happy Valentine's Day Rox-Ann, who Turns us On with her Special Frown. "You should smile," Marvin says, smiling. Bill holds his hands out to me. "The telephone did ring," Dixie says.

I pick it up.

"Roxanne?"

"Max, are you all right?"

"Leave your car at work and I'll pick you up."

"What for?" I say.

"Roxanne, hang up," Edna says.

Bill looks at me and shakes his head. He buttons his coat, drinks his beer down fast, and leaves. The door swings behind him.

"Roxanne?" Max says.

I look around at the bar, the dingy walls, the flyspecked ceil-ing, my patrons lined up and smiling like for a photo. Max says, "I'll come out, drink a beer with you and shoot some pool, and afterwards take you out for eggs." I look at the banner above me, the lopsided heart around my misspelled name. "Roxanne," Max says, "let's give it a try." It's a small gesture. It arrives on time.

Starbuck

I heard the explosion that killed Bo.

The next thing I knew, Tad Lee needed formula because my milk was gone. Jewel hung on my leg. I smelled Bo's smell. And one day, a few weeks later, bent over mopping, I felt a hand on my neck and heard Bo say, clear as day, my name. When I came to, Jewel was leaning over me. I asked the doctor for Valiums. With some of the insurance money I bought a trailer and made Mama live in it in my yard. Soon, though, I stayed at the trailer and she took the house with the kids because I was working nights and, by then, selling speed.

That's how it was.

And I was shooting pool at the Dark Moon with my cousin Billy, and a man with a chain connecting his belt to his wallet and a bird tattoo on each arm said, "Let's play partners. Get your friend a partner."

He was called Tom.

"Should I get rid of him?" Billy asked. I was the best shot there.

A few weeks later, in a different bar, Billy and I told Tom how, last year, in a mood because I'd paid cash for a TransAm, we drove to Memphis on Christmas and checked into a hotel to drink. And Billy passed out in his oatmeal in the cafe and he was heavy so I left him there and the front desk called my room to get me to move him, and I tried but only got him to the lobby and left him on a couch for a few more hours, oatmeal smeared on his face. And then we went home and Billy's family and mine, watching the

Rose Bowl on TV, wouldn't talk to us. His daddy still won't talk to me.

"That's sick," Tom said.

Billy looked up, his eyebrows in a frown.

I said, "What?"

"You traveling around together."

"Maybe you don't understand," I said.

"And what are you saying I don't understand?" He was hanging onto the edge of the table and he reached over to pinch my face hard.

"Sex," I said.

But he knew something. First night we were together he did things so strange that, had I been asked, I would have said no. But I buckled down and matched him. "Ava," he said, when it was done, "my Angel, my Squeeze." And I made him comb his hair so when he walked down the driveway and past the house Mama wouldn't realize he'd just got out of bed.

"When two people who are cousins fuck each other," Tom said, smoke whirling up, "they don't admit it."

I slapped him.

He hit me. Then Billy hit him, I think, and drove me to Emergency.

Tom left fast, his motorcycle wheels spitting. I put a warrant out.

He called the next day.

"Ava," he said. "You sent the police after me."

"My nose is broke."

"I didn't hit you hard," he said.

I said, "You had the right to slap me, but not to hit me."

He said, "It's just that when I thought about you and him being together I saw red."

I hung up.

The telephone rang again and I took it off the hook and sat

there thinking, about Bo who, the entire time I knew him, from when I was sixteen until I was twenty when he died, was late for something, messed up, buckling his pants on the way out the door because of me—and me, lazy, a bad housekeeper, dwelling on the last time Bo and I did it, when we would next, and how: candles burning, a fan whirling over the bed, hot, perfumey oil making us slick.

I got my babies like that, not planned.

Since then I've had Fred, big and fat, who needs his sleep. Someone else who was predictable, more excited than me. It lasted two minutes, my trigger never tripped. But I said to myself: Ava, Bo is not returning, make do. And Tom came, wiry as lightning.

I walked up the driveway to Mama's house. "It throws me to see tape on your nose," she said. She had her apron tied around her waist which, because she is big and doesn't stand up straight, meshes into her bosom. A chicken was laying on the counter and I picked it up and yanked it open and ran cold water through.

"How did your nose get broke?" she said.

"Someone hit me."

She said, "What did you say so someone hit you?"

I was being polite. "Are you keeping these guts?" I said.

She said, "I've seen some man at the trailer and I'm old-fashioned but I know something bad when I see it, and I think of Bo and get sick."

I said, "You didn't like Bo when he wasn't dead."

"Maybe not," she said. "I smell trouble."

I stood in front of her, set the chicken down. I wiped my hands, put them in her apron pockets. "When payday comes," I said, "I'll take you to Fayetteville and buy you that antique doll."

She said, "Ava?"

"What?"

"Who is he?"

"Nobody."

"Ava."

"Tom Starbuck," I said. "But he's not coming around."

That was Thursday. On Saturday I put the kids in the car to go to town and get them haircuts and, a mile down the road, Tom's motorcycle pulled out of a pasture and he dogged me until I stopped. I rolled down my window. "You're going to get arrested," I said.

He pulled his sunglasses off. "Are those your kids, Ava? Hey, I never saw them before. How are you, boy?" He said this to Jewel.

I tied her shoe.

He got off his bike. "Call off the cops," he said.

In front of the sun, which was red and sinking, his face looked white. I mean, the bones glowed. "Are you getting enough to eat?" I asked.

He said, "Get rid of the cops."

I drove away.

That night when my digital clock said 12:17, a shadow crossed it. A hand touched my face. "I'm crazy about you," he said.

"Go away," I said.

He told me flat, "I didn't do anything wrong."

"You did."

He said, "Then it's between you and me, no one else."

It was pitch dark. "What made you decide you were crazy about me?" I asked. I pictured my heart: red, hard. And I thought suddenly of Bo's junked car I had hauled away that day. I sat up.

"Go away," I said.

Tom laid down.

The light through the window made curly shadows on his face. "The feeling I have," he said, "hurts." He clenched his hands together. He lifted up my nightgown and put his head underneath it. "Drop the charges," he said, kissing, his voice buried, muffled.

My eyes were closed and this time I saw Bo dead: black as dirt, his eyes and teeth white.

"Squeeze," Tom said, "be with me now."

I opened my eyes.

"I won't drop the charges," I said.

Tom said, "The law does not stop me from hitting you. Love does. Besides, you sell speed for money, what do you want with cops?"

"Speed," I said, "I mean to give up."

We crossed the state line and I reached to pull the keys out of the ignition. "I'll lose my job," I said. That was one reason. "I can't leave my kids," I said. "It would break me apart."

Tom pushed me away.

"You won't need a job where we're going."

My fingernails ripped as I grabbed the sleeve of his jacket. "You can't haul me away in my car," I said.

He pushed the accelerator down.

"I just did."

We rented an ugly place in Wichita and Tom bought me a ring, a microwave oven, a patchwork rabbit-fur jacket, and a color TV. I thought always of Jewel and Tad Lee, and Mama, who wouldn't let them come to the phone when I called.

"Squeeze," Tom said, "I've done for you what I could."

It was afternoon. We were on the edge of town in a cold field looking for arrowheads.

"I hate where we live," I said.

"We'll move."

I said, "Jewel's starting school next year. I want to be there."

He said, "But haven't you pictured us together, forever?" He stood behind me, arms around me, hands on my tits. I said, "I've had Jewel since I was sixteen and Tad Lee since I was nineteen, but you since May."

"What binds us together is different."

"I want my kids," I said.

He said, "You feel torn up? You don't want to be apart?"

He ripped my blouse.

"That's how I feel about you."

And we did it right there in the mud and he stood up afterwards and put his underwear on and said, "Go ahead, send for your kids."

We drove to a phone booth. I was wearing Tom's shirt. He was bare-chested in the car. "Mama?" I said. "Is Jewel still coughing?"

She said, "Why don't you come find out?"

I said, "I am coming but it's to get the kids and bring them here."

She started crying.

"We'll work something out," I said.

That night, frying hamburger, I asked Tom, "Where will we live when the kids come?" He opened the newspaper. "Away from white trash," he said.

The new house was six miles out, with tall ceilings and big windows. Our landlord, fussy about who we were and if we'd be good tenants, said, "This old home is where I was born and I hope you'll be respectful."

Tom looked at me. He opened a window. "Old man," he said, "when you get to know us, you'll be amazed."

A truck delivered crates the next day.

"Surprise," Tom said, pulling a rooster out. "And hens too."

The rooster sat on Tom's arm and Tom said, "A rooster doesn't like a hen and a hen doesn't like a rooster, but what can they do?" I had a misgiving then. And we went fishing and Tom found a clam and ripped it open and threw the meat out on the rock, like to let it rot. I said, "Why, when you won't eat it?" He said, "Because a clam is a thing that, cleaned out, makes a nice doo-daw."

That night I counted the bones in his back. "I knew you would be happy," he said, his face in the pillow, wind wafting the curtains high and lofty.

"I'm worried about Mama," I said.

"She's not coming too."

"Why won't you let her come?"

"I'm letting your kids come," he said, "that's enough."

He went to sleep and I went downstairs and called Mama. "I'm trying to get you here," I said.

She said, "You haven't been right for years."

I said, "I'm trying to do for you."

She said "What's wrong with you?"

I told her how I'd fallen in the river that day and my tailbone, which she knows cracked when I had Tad Lee, ached and pained. She cried. I said, "Why do you sling snot every time I call?"

She blew her nose. "He pushed you," she said.

I said, "The change of life has made you crazy."

She hung up.

I stood there and thought about how problems crop up fast and people say they saw them coming but no one warns you. And a gun went off.

I looked out the window.

Tom was naked, aiming at a tree. I went on the porch. "I couldn't sleep," he said, walking over. He laid the gun down and opened my robe. He said, "You're good-looking and good to get at."

I said, "This concerns the future, Tom."

He said, "If it's about your Mama, no. I'm letting your kids come, that's enough."

I said, "When I go pick them up I'll have to stay and ease her through."

Mama ran down the driveway towards my car as its wheels crunched over the gravel driveway at home, her big arms and legs flying. I hugged her and we went inside and she fried pork chops while I gave Tad Lee his bottle, and Jewel stood on a stool and combed my hair.

I said, "The house seems dark."

She said, "It's that time of year."

"Did you rent the trailer?"

She said, "Billy stays in it."

"Does he give you money?"

She said, "You should worry about money."

She poured flour in a pan. "I can't live with you and a man."

I said, "You don't know him."

"I know what he looks like."

"You didn't like Bo at first," I said.

She said, "He was a grown man and you were a girl."

I said, "Tom is making us a home."

She threw dough on the cutting board. "And how did he like you coming here without him?"

Something crashed against the door. I opened it slowly. "Billy?"

Tom stepped out into the light. "I should've known," he said.

I said, "Why are you here?"

"I hitchhiked. I came back to get my bike."

I said, "Come meet Mama."

"No thank you."

"Who is it?" Mama said.

Tom said, "I'm warning you."

"Get him out of here," Mama said.

Tom said, "Go ahead. Call the police. That's your way."

That night I sat in the trailer. A pair of Bo's coveralls hung on the wall, limp, a hard hat over them, those clothes waiting, I felt, for something living or dead to fill them. I opened the window and, rain beating down, called for Tom. "Please," I said.

He came inside and a few minutes later, spent, naked, pacing and smacking his fists against his thighs, he said, "Why do you torture me?"

I said, "Me?"

There was a knock at the door. "Police," they said. "Open up."

I pushed Tom in a back room and threw his clothes in after him. I sent the officer away by saying, "Ever since Daddy died, every time it rains since Daddy died, Mama sees something in the yard that turns out to be nothing." I shut the door. I was looking at those coveralls again when I considered that my trouble was not Tom, not Bo, but the fact of Billy who Tom says I've been with. "I'm not smart but neither am I blind," Tom said to me once. I said, "I never got laid by Billy." Tom said, "Well, not lately."

I never got laid by Billy.

I opened the back bedroom door and Tom was climbing out a window.

"Own up," he said, "before trouble comes down."

Mama said, "Love stands a test."

I threw a plastic tumbler against the wall.

"Shit and piss," I said. And Tom pulled up in the yard and gunned his motorcycle.

Mama ran in circles, then grabbed a baseball bat and went outside on the porch. She said, "If you harm one hair on one of our heads, one hair on one head, I'll kill you."

Tom said, "Ava and I got business yet."

I packed.

Mama stood over me as I threw things in suitcases and shopping bags and she said I wasn't fit for a mother and I don't want my kids. This isn't true. Tad Lee was small for a trip, I decided, and Jewel had that cough.

"Billy's here," Mama said.

"Billy," I hollered out the window, "put my luggage rack on."

Outside, pulling on the straps on the rack he was putting on my car, Billy said, "Your mama called mine just now to say she was hauling you to the state hospital and needed help." I put my hands on my hips and said, loud enough for Mama, "There's one crazy person in this family and she's fat."

She was standing on the porch with that baseball bat. She said, "We could send you away if we wanted, Ava, and that's a fact."

Driving back to Wichita, I ate speed.

I was on the road seven hours.

I pulled into the yard and the landlord stood on the porch and mopped his face and said, "Where have you been? There's bullet holes in the house." I got out and walked around to the back. The chickens were dead: red and white, feathers and blood. I can't stand a mess. I picked up the shovel and stopped to think where to dig a hole and Tom appeared, naked from the waist up, the wings of his tattoos spread.

"I came into your life fast," he said, "and now I'm going out."

He hit me.

I laid on my back and looked at the sky, wide and white, the trees shining silver, ropes of leaves twinkling and bird's wings flapping like crescent moons. Sore is what I felt: also clean. Away, away. The motorcycle roared. "I never got his name," the landlord said from the door.

This Far North

I woke up and my first impulse was to get my ice auger and tip-ups out of the closet and go to the lake. I lay there and thought about bait, about the shelter I built which stays dark and warm, though outside the hills and drifts are so brilliant they hurt my eyes. Inside, a pale, chilly light passes through the floor, which is really the frozen lake. But this was no ordinary Saturday, no fishing day; Patience wasn't beside me. She'd spent the night at her grandma's, to feel like a virgin again for one day, to best startle me with her whiteness as she appeared in a puff of gauze at the church.

So I walked into the living room where my mother and two sisters and niece were sleeping on the floor in front of the fire. I saw the clutter and cringed: clothes, toys, a diaper unfurling in my best chair. I took a deep breath, pulled the belt of my bathrobe tight, and said, "We should make breakfast."

Iris sat up. "Hello, Uncle Vernon," she said. She ran towards me, put her arms around me, rubbed my chest, and kissed my hair and ears, though I hadn't had my shower yet. She's Wendy's four-year-old. Wendy's not doing a good job with her. My other sister, Marianne, sat up and blinked, her eyes tiny and rimmed with eyelashes so blond that, without makeup, they look transparent. Patience met my sisters last night. "How will they act?" she asked. And, more to the point, "Are they like your father?"

Wendy stood up and stretched. "Where's Prudence?" she asked.

"She means Patience," my mother said.

The telephone rang. I picked it up. "Hello?"

"Vernon."

"Hello, Johnette," I said.

She said, "It's your wedding day."

"I know."

"I had to come."

"I said no. I'll talk to you later." I hung up.

"Is she coming?" Marianne asked.

"Of course not."

"Her mother was acquitted," my mother said.

Marianne was standing in the kitchen, with a coffee can and a plastic measuring spoon. She set them both on the counter and turned around. "What was Johnette's mother acquitted for?" she said.

"She shot her husband," Mother said. "He used to beat her, and he tried to set her hair on fire and she shot him later, when he was in bed."

Marianne's eyes opened wide. "How terrible. What did Johnette say?"

I said, "We were broke up by then."

"Why can't she come to your wedding?"

"Think of Patience," I said. "Use your head."

"Think of Johnette," Marianne said. "Use yours."

I met Johnette two years ago when she pulled in the filling station I worked at in a convertible that had been primed, not painted. I cleaned the windshield and watched the way she moved her gum when she chewed, her chest rising and falling under her peach-colored T-shirt when she sang with the radio. Her hair, which was dark at the roots, had seemed like a mystery to me then. "I'll paint your car for you cheap," I said. She wanted it red with flecks. I thought white would be classy. We painted it blue and when it was done—looking cherry—she gave me a key on a foot-long golden ornament, her named carved in curly letters: Johnette.

My first lay. My year-long mistake.

Marianne looked out the window. "Where's your Camaro, Vernon?"

"I traded it."

"For what?"

My station wagon is brown; the rust hardly shows. "I got a deal," I said.

"You quit racing," Marianne said.

I didn't answer. I was doing the dishes from last night. I was thinking of the time I'd taken Johnette to a family picnic at the lake and, kneeling in the driver's seat in a red bikini, her streaky hair like a banner behind her, she slammed the speedboat into high waves at dangerous angles. We pulled up to the dock where my father waited, drink in hand. He looked at Johnette: top, bottom. He said, "This is your who?" He wanted an introduction. I led her back to the picnic table and made her wear my mother's beachrobe.

"Settled down," Marianne said.

I looked up. "Pardon me?"

Wendy was holding a smoking curling iron close to her head.

Iris was smearing food on the table.

Marianne said, "Settled down isn't something you decide to do, Vernon."

I picked up the keys to my car. I said, "I'll go for a drive and take Iris."

Marianne said, "It decides on you."

At the motel I helped Iris out of the car and, holding her hand in mine, knocked on my father's door. "Hello," I said. I knocked louder.

"Come on in," he yelled.

He was sitting in bed, bare-chested, the covers to his waist, his arm around Scootie, who was wearing a pink nightgown. She's been his girlfriend for a few months, he says. A few years is accurate, but he's only been living away from my mother for a few months. Iris jumped on the bed. "Hello, Granddaddy," she said. She kissed him, stroked his face. He hadn't shaved or combed his hair yet.

"Is the room okay?" I looked around. A bottle of Christian Brothers sat on the nightstand.

Scootie stood up and zipped into a robe the same color as her hair: orange-red. "There's no hot water," she said, "and one bar of soap has been chewed on by mice. I'm going to call the manager."

She held her arms out to me.

Patience says that until my father marries Scootie we should only be civil.

Scootie went to see my mother once to tell her that she was my father's lover and there'd been others: the piano teacher, the chiropractor's receptionist, my old baby-sitter named Ginger. My mother said it was untrue, my father was impotent, had been for years. She hit Scootie. Then Father left Mother and came back on Easter, quiet and ashamed. He made love to her on the living room floor at midnight, saying it was going to be all right now. That's what she says. She baked his favorite pie, peach. He left again.

"Vernon," Scootie said, her arms still outstretched to me. "This day belongs to you and Patience and don't let anyone spoil it."

I hugged her back.

My father sat up in bed. "Hey, on the way here," he said, "Vernon, the travel trailer came unhitched and started to roll away and was pulling the whole van off the road. And I stopped and got the trailer hitched up, and it started to roll away again when we were driving through this small town. And then a shopping cart blew off a grocery store parking lot and into the side of the damn van."

Scootie said, "It's a sign, I tell you. Bad times ahead."

My father rolled his eyes. "She watches TV preachers," he said, "*and* swears by newspaper horoscopes." He pulled the curtain back from the window, pointed at my car and said, "Is that your junk?"

I said, "Yes."

He said, "No more racing."

"Right."

He sighed. "All that money wasted. If Marianne would have been a boy she would've raced—cars, motorcycles, snowmobiles. If she would have raced," he said, "she would have kept her pants on."

Iris pulled his chest hairs.

"Ouch," he said. "Now why does she do that?"

She reached and pulled them again. "I love you, Granddaddy," she said.

In the church basement Marianne pinned a boutonniere on my lapel. "Iris has a strange way of expressing love," she said. She shrugged, leaned close, and asked me, "How long have you known Patience?"

"Well, you should talk," I said. Marianne ran away with Bert when she was seventeen, after having known him two weeks. He was in town with a construction crew from Texas, which is where they live now, and since then they've split up and reconciled three times.

"I just love Bert," Marianne said, "and the way he looks in cowboy boots." She stared at my face, her eyelashes thick with mascara. She said, "Every man I get excited about is hot-tempered."

I said, "Patience cooks big meals every night and I wash the dishes and, afterwards, do crossword puzzles or watch TV while she sews."

Marianne said, "We can blame that on Mother."

I said, "What?"

She said, "The way you act now."

It's true that after everyone left, first Marianne, then Wendy, then Father, I stayed at the house with Mother for a year. She used to chase me down the driveway yelling my socks didn't match. She made slipcovers for the seats in my Camaro. And I moved away and she came to visit every weekend. Once she vowed not to: "I don't want to be a burden," she said over the phone. I found her in my driveway the next day, when the thermometer said twenty-six below. I was cold, and I was in my work clothes, long johns, coveralls. I took her inside. Johnette said, "You're looking well, Doris." Mother was thin, but her clothes and jewelry were new. Johnette took Mother's steamed-up glasses and cleaned them. "Your eyes are pretty," she said, "you should get contacts." She painted Mother's eyelids blue and held a mirror up. Mother blinked. Johnette threw the mirror on the floor. She started crying, not Mother. "Goddamn," she said. Mother blinked again.

"I don't want that," I told Marianne.

She said, "What?"

I said, "Someone who acts weak under pressure."

Marianne stopped combing my hair. "Then you need someone who's had experience with it," she said. The church bell was ringing.

Patience moved up the aisle while I waited. Flashcubes flared, a child cried, but her face remained the same, frozen. "She's scared," her brother, Merle, said when he handed her to me.

The minister asked her to repeat after him and she didn't.

"I, Patience, take you, Vernon . . ." he prompted a second time.

I nudged her. I pinched her arm.

"I, Patience, take you, Vernon," she said at last.

We were pelted with rice.

My father stood up. "I want Scootie in the family picture," he said. "If Scootie's not in the family picture, then I won't be either."

I looked at Patience. I looked at Mother, her bowed head. Would she cry? She reached out and straightened Iris's sash. I breathed deeply, stared at the blue picture of Jesus above the altar.

"I don't want to be in the family picture," Scootie said, quietly.

My father said, "You're family to me."

"Dad," I said, "after the family picture is taken, we'll have another one: you and Scootie, me and Patience, just the four of us."

"All right," he said. He sat down.

On the sidewalk, on the way into the reception, I held Patience's hand.

"The golf course looks strange," she said. "I've always pictured green, green for my reception."

"Snow is pretty," I said. I led her inside. I asked her, "Are you all right?" She didn't eat or drink. She looked frail in the bell-shaped dress she'd picked out. The scalloped veil framed her face, which is lightly freckled. Her hair is pale, nearly white.

"Who are these people?" she said.

Patience has lived all her life in this small town I moved to last year. Johnette came with me but there were fights. I didn't care, she said. I cared. She cried every day and I couldn't make her stop. Love would make her stop, she said, if she got enough.

Finally, I wanted it quiet. She moved away.

Patience cut my hair at the only beauty parlor or barbershop in town. When I spoke to her, she blushed. The next day I asked her out.

Patience said, "Who are the ugly little girls with scratches on their faces?"

"My cousins," I said, "twins. They fight a lot."

My father focused his camera. His drink spilled and he reached to pick it up, dropped the camera. Scootie sat there and frowned.

My mother twirled, making her striped skirt swirl. "Wendy," she said, "I'm having schnapps on the rocks."

Wendy was whispering to Marianne. Marianne nodded, her slip hanging below her dress.

Iris danced with Mother.

"Scootie," my father said, shaking his camera, "I can't get this thing to work."

"Is your father having fun?" Patience's grandmother asked me this.

I didn't have time to answer.

It was like the crowd parted and there Johnette was, lips full and wet, her shoulders thrown back. She was wearing a red dress. She smiled. "Congratulations," she said.

Patience said, "Who is it?"

I crossed the room. Iris ran up to me, grabbed my hand and kissed it.

"What are you doing" I asked Johnette.

She said, "I had to come."

"Scootie," my father yelled.

My mother came over. "Vernon, honey. I'm going home now." She hung on my arm. Her eyes widened. "Johnette, sweetie," she said, "you're here." She kissed her, hugged her, then walked away.

Johnette turned to me. "Vernon, you said you'd call."

I watched Patience maneuvering her wide skirts across the room, through the bathroom door. "I'll walk you to your car," I said.

Iris bit my hand.

"Quit it," I said, and I wiped it on my pants.

Iris started to cry. "But I love you, Uncle Vernon," she said.

Johnette stopped smiling. "Forget it," she said. She put her coat on and one sleeve flew up and hit me in the face. She walked away.

"Goddamn it all to hell," my father said.

Scootie said, "We should get him out of here."

"No," he said.

"Vernon," Scootie said, "help me."

We got him outside, and Scootie said, "Put your coat on and get in the car."

"Take it easy, old-timer," someone said.

He slipped, almost fell.

He swayed, made a move to put his hands in his pockets, but the camera strap got in his way. "Goddamn it," he said. "I paid a fortune for this and I don't even know how to use it." He pulled the camera off his neck and threw it over his shoulder into the snow.

Scootie's breath came out in even measures, white puffs. "If you don't get in this car," she said, "I will, and I'll leave you here."

"Fat chance," he said. "It's my car."

She turned to leave.

He rushed at her, held one arm behind her back, and reached for the keys.

"Someone help me," she yelled. "Help!"

I hesitated. I do help women, but this was different.

My father knocked the keys out of her hand.

I picked them up.

"Give them to me," Scootie said. She had him pinned against the car with one knee. "Vernon, give the keys to me," she said. She reached and grabbed me by my lapels, then slapped me.

I gave the keys to her.

I was aware of Patience behind me, the swish of her dress.

A car roared out of the parking lot. I looked up: Johnette's.

Scootie shoved my father onto the ground and got in the car.

He stood up, lunged for the door handle, hung on.

"Daddy, stop!" Marianne yelled, running after him. She grabbed him.

"Marianne, you stop!" I yelled.

She dug her heels in the snow. "Goddamn it," she said, "I'm helping."

"All of you, stop," I yelled, "stop!"

Marianne let go of Father.

He let go of the car and slid to the ground.

He lay there, staring at the fading taillights. He put his hand on Marianne's leg. "Good," he said, "good girl."

"Where's Patience?" I asked.

"Christ," Marianne said.

I looked up.

The golf course is bordered with tall, spiky pine trees, which look black at night. The stars were twinkling and, beneath them, I saw Patience sinking past her knees in snow, staggering through it. She stopped on a hill a quarter-mile away and panted, her dress billowing. A gust of wind lifted her veil into the sky.

Patience's grandmother walked up. "Go get Patience," she said. She was talking to Patience's brother, Merle.

"I'll go," I said.

Merle said, "She's scared. Come by and get her in the morning."

"Wait a minute," I said, "I'm her husband."

"You'll wait," he said, "and that's it."

"Vernon."

I turned around.

Marianne and Father were standing behind me, and Wendy and Iris.

"We need a ride," Marianne said.

I should have been on my way to the honeymoon suite in the Dells. I pushed the gas pedal down, balloons around my feet, tin cans clanking behind me. I dropped my sisters and Iris off at my place first, then drove my father to the motel. I pulled into the parking lot.

"You think it was my fault," he said.

"I wish it hadn't happened," I said.

He said, "You never did anything exciting in your life."

I didn't answer.

"You're like her," he said, "scared to take a chance, scared of living."

"Who?" I said. I had no idea. He used to say these things about me and Mother.

He scratched his head. "Scootie, I guess. I wish Marianne was a boy."

I reached over and opened his door. I said, "Is everything okay?"

He shrugged, walked to the motel room. He turned around. "Hey, I paid for the goddamn room," he yelled, suddenly. I held my breath but the door opened and, a few minutes later, the lights went out.

At home, Wendy and Marianne were leaning over Mother, who

was lying on her back on the hallway floor. "We found her here," Marianne said.

"Is she all right?"

"She's drunk," Wendy said.

"I'm not," Mother said. She showed me a jar of cold cream. "I'm taking off my makeup. Vernon, why are you here? Where's Patience?"

"Sick," Marianne said.

"What's wrong with her?"

"She's sick," Marianne said.

Then she reminded us of the time I'd fallen down the stairs and Dad was at a bar with the car and couldn't be found, and Mother fainted. Marianne pulled me to the clinic in the toy wagon. "You kept saying you were fine," she said, "but your leg was broken and bleeding." I remembered it. My leg had hurt but Marianne was crying, so I stayed calm. At the hospital she kissed me, got snot and water on my face, and said, "Tomorrow will be a better day."

"Go to bed," I said.

They spread their sleeping bags on the floor while I straightened the house. Then, when the only sound coming from the living room was the sound of my family sleeping, I got warm clothes and fishing gear out of the closet and went to the lake. I didn't sit in my shelter this time but outside, next to the fire. I watched the wood become coal, smoke spiraling upward into blackness, and I thought about Patience, her veil hovering above her: white, static. The fire faded and the sky grew pale. I waited for a sign, a streak of pink telling me it was time to get her and bring her home. I was cold while I waited but I waited. Winter is my season.

The Widower's Psalm

She was fifteen years and seven months old and a man named Harlan came up with a construction crew from Texas to work on the water tower. Even the grown women talked about Harlan, how debonair he was in the coffee shop, how he shot pool like a shark. He kept a silver three-toned travel trailer on the edge of town. After his car skidded into a telephone pole one night and he was instantly killed folks went inside the trailer to find out who his kin were so they could send for them. They found good liquor, gold satin sheets on the bed, and a photo of Harlan lying on those sheets, bare-chested, hands behind his head.

That's the photo they put in the paper.

But Harlan was twenty-two and Linda wasn't sixteen yet when he climbed the water tower and painted LINDA ON MY MIND, the name of the Conway Twitty song, in six-foot letters on the side. He got fired and ran out of money and that was the way he came to end his days in Cherryvale. The water tower stayed like that until they tore it down: a robin's-egg blue cylinder jutting into the sky on spindly legs with black and uneven letters curving around it. Linda's stepfather beat her the morning he first looked up and saw her name there, then locked her in the shed for three days. Everyone knew. She was the only Linda in town.

I was delivering newspapers when I first saw her. She was leaping through the sprinkler in the front yard to her ramshackle, unpainted house. She was wearing a red plaid swimsuit and water glistened in beads on her legs and her ponytail hung like a rope on her back. Her family never paid for the paper but I delivered it anyway.

Sometimes, in the attic of their shed, I laid in a pile of hay while she rubbed slivers of ice on my chest. (She was the nurse and I was the soldier.) Then Sammy Manwell moved to town and she tended his wounds, not mine. She sent me away to fetch things and drive the enemy back, and when I returned she and Sammy were gone from the haystack and the spot where they'd been laying when I left was flattened out. I kissed her once, between the LP gas tank and the cellar stairs, and she asked me for money for gum.

I was with Sammy one day when she stood on her back steps in a white dress and said she'd recently come to realize what love was and it wasn't what she had with Sammy. He ran his bicycle into a tree. She loved several movie stars, the man who ran the Ferris wheel at the fair, the doctor when she had the mumps, Harlan when she was fifteen.

The summer I turned sixteen Sammy was in Wichita working at his uncle's store and Linda and I rode our bikes to Pilgrim's Creek and laid on a flat rock underneath the limbs of a wide oak tree. She unhooked my overall straps, one at a time, then peeled my clothes away. I lay naked on the rock and she bent down and delicately kissed the tip of my pecker, which seemed red and strong and spear-shaped to me then. She guided my hand underneath her skirt to the inside of her cotton pants. "Sherm," she said, "see? This part of me always stays cool."

On prom night the year Sammy and I were seniors and Linda was fourteen she wore a dress made of coral-colored shiny material with little yellow beaded pineapples on it and her cleavage showed plump and neat and the earrings in her ears sparkled bright as her front tooth, which was silver.

My date was Arleen Sanders.

The four of us stayed at prom long enough to dance only a few times beneath the swirled crepe paper on the gymnasium ceiling and Linda said we should go to her house because her stepfather was gone and she had the key to the cabinet where he stored the liquor. He was always gone on Saturdays. We drank choke-cherry juice mixed with Southern Comfort, slices of orange floating in the tall glasses, and Linda turned the radio up loud. She dabbed whiskey behind her ears and on her wrists. She lifted up her skirt and dabbed whiskey behind her knees like it was perfume.

I was in the front room on a dark green, prickly sofa kissing Arleen when Linda's stepfather burst in, ran to Linda's bedroom door, and yanked it open. Linda stood with her eyes wide, arms in an *X* across her chest. Then she reached for her dress, unzipped and hanging around her waist, and held it to her as she ran through the front room and out the door. Sammy followed, tucking his shirt in his pants.

Linda's stepfather threw rocks at the car as we sped down the driveway. He yelled, "Whore!" Arleen had to be in by midnight so we took her home. Linda cried for a while. Then she and Sammy and I drove to Pilgrim's Creek and sat on the rock and watched the water crash. The moon shone like a disk on the creek's surface and Linda stood up. "I'm going swimming," she said.

Sammy said it wasn't warm enough.

I said we didn't have any swimsuits.

Linda said, "I'm going in wearing my skivvies." She unzipped her dress and dove in wearing her white underpants and her bra with its old-fashioned cone-shaped cups. "Scaredy cats," she yelled, treading water.

Sammy and I stood on the rock, Sammy wearing a blue sportscoat, holding the bottle of Southern Comfort. I hung my clothes on a tree and dove in after Linda. An hour later the three of us walked upstream and waded out to the ledge where the water fell.

"I know it's deep enough down there," Linda said, "if we jump in the middle and not to the left and not to the right. And if we don't try to dive."

She jumped first, disappearing, then reemerging and shooting downstream. We all jumped many times: the current expelled us, then transported us away. But when Linda leapt into that pocket of water for the last time Sammy reached out to pat her on the hips. He reached to pat her in that split second when she was not on the ledge and not plummeting into water, but poised in air.

She landed facing the falls.

Sammy and I watched her flail. We watched her long mahogany-colored hair spiral, spiral around slowly, then faster, then faster and faster. "What the hell is going on?" Sammy yelled. "What's she doing?" He dove in after her.

She reached for him and by the force of that exertion slid out of the eddy. He slid in. I watched her float downstream. And I watched him struggle and jumped in after him. I hung onto a rock with one hand and with the other I pulled him out. We drifted downstream and Linda clung to a branch. "Help me," she said. "I'm tired."

She laid on the pebble-covered beach then, her chest heaving, and we kneeled over her. "I was ready to give myself up to that underwater grave, Sammy," she said, "and your white arm flashed by in the green water and I decided to live."

A man came by to fish that morning and was so frightened by the sight of the three of us wet and bedraggled on the creek bank that he drove to a phone and called the police. The sun was high and we passed delivery trucks and farmers on tractors as we rode back to town in the squad car. Linda got locked in the shed for three weeks. Sammy got sent to Wichita to live with his uncle. Everyone was sure he'd be a basketball star there but one night he got drunk and broke into an ice cream parlor that showed coin-operated dirty movies and he stole some bags of quarters. In the morning, sober, he went to return the money and the police, waiting for him there, arrested him.

When Linda was fifteen Arleen Sanders said, "You don't advertise something that's not for sale." Linda had just walked past wearing a halter she'd made by tying two blue bandannas together.

Linda's voice was soft and pretty but when she got drunk it was raspy; and before, when she said mean things, it was accidental but now it wasn't. We were standing around a pickup with a keg in the back, and in front of eight or ten people she said to Arleen, "If I had a bladder the size of yours I'd give up beer and wouldn't try to act like I was putting on lipstick every time I walked around the corner to pee." To me she said, "Sherm, you wear that same damn green-checked shirt every Saturday night. Can't you spring for something new?"

Then Harlan came to town and I ran into Linda every Saturday night and most weeknights at the corner tap, My Place it was called. Harlan had convinced the owner to let her in and most of the time she sat on a barstool talking to him while Harlan shot pool. She smoked cigarettes, drank a shot of whiskey every fourth beer. Every drink the owner didn't pay for, Harlan did. Or I did, sometimes.

One afternoon when I didn't have to work and Linda had less inclination than usual to go to school we decided to drive to Pilgrim's Creek. I pulled up in front of her house in my truck and she burst out the door and tottered down the sidewalk in a one-piece swimsuit and heels, carrying a straw bag. We sat on the rock and she painted her toenails and said Harlan wanted to marry her and his grandmother was going to give them her farm and move to an old folks home. She said, "And when I get that place and make it mine I'm not going to pick one color for my decor. I'll put in it everything of every color that strikes me pretty, and if I put enough colors together—red, blue, pink, gray, yellow—it'll all match. Doesn't that sound nice?"

Harlan climbed the water tower that weekend and was killed in that crash before Linda's stepfather let her out of the shed. My boss's wife—I was pumping gas then—told me about that photo of Harlan they put in the paper and where it came from. They'd found photos of Linda lying wrapped in those gold bedsheets too.

So Linda quit school and worked at the Mercantile. She dated the salesmen who came to town and one of them took a picture of her dressed in clothes from the line he sold, a picture I still have: her hair coiled high, wearing a satin dress and pearls, she holds a seashell.

I asked her to go to the harvest dance with me and the weather turned cold and we stood on the sidewalk and watched people drinking and twirling around in the blocked-off street. Sammy Manwell appeared. "Sammy," Linda called. She ran into the street to meet him. He looked heavier than he used to and he had a beard that was darker than the hair on his head and he looked sloppy. His shirt wasn't tucked in his pants. "You came back," she said.

And the three of us sat on a bench at the end of the street and I asked Sammy where he'd been. In jail, he said, serving time for possession of marijuana with intent to sell.

Linda said, "But did you smoke it?"

He passed us a joint. It was my first, Linda's too. "God," she said. She held her head in her hands between her legs and her hair spread like a fan on the grass. She said, "Sherm, don't let me drive." She stuffed her keys up my sleeve between my wrist and coat cuff.

The neon cross on top of the Presbyterian church glowed. Sammy said, "Think of what that must have cost—the cross, I mean."

Linda said, "It did cost a lot. I heard."

Sammy said, "They could have spent the money planting food. Or getting ready for the nuclear fallout."

Linda said, "But it's so pretty. Don't you think so, Sherm?"

Sammy said, "It's a monument to the human belief that what lies ahead is an improvement."

I walked away. I went downtown and danced with Arleen Sanders until my shirt stuck to my back and sweat streamed down my face from under my hat, and then I followed her home and made love to her in her trailer. "Finally," she said. She fell asleep with her head on my chest and I looked out the window, at the driveway, the streetlight and, beyond that, the flat horizon and the starless sky.

I drove home at four and one of those storms, where the snow falls lightly and dusts the edge of the road and the sagebrush white, was just beginning. I found Linda huddled in the doorway to a downtown store, her skinny, nyloned legs looking cold below her parka, smashed paper cups, food wrappers, and napkins strewn around her. Harlan once said to me, "She's so unspoiled, a small-town girl." And when we were in high school Sammy said he loved Linda because she seemed older than him. My father said, before he died, "A pretty girl is everything everyone wants her to be." Also, "You have a claim when you stake it."

I married Linda right away. "We'll hang a cowbell on the bedsprings and wait outside the window to hear it ring," someone yelled. A flash went off in my face. Everyone was drunk. We drove to the motel. The wedding night was not what it should have been.

I was working at the gas station then and I got so dirty every day that it took me a half an hour to clean up and my hands and fingernails never came clean. It seemed right that Linda should quit her job at the Mercantile, but we didn't have enough money so I took a second job in a small building on the edge of town. I'd passed by that building all my life and wondered what kind of business they did. They collected bills. It was my job to go around in dress pants and a good shirt and tell people to pay a little every month if they couldn't pay the whole thing.

Sometimes Linda had dinner waiting for me. I knew most everyone whose door I knocked on. And when I came home at night I was tired and didn't want to talk. I sat on the porch of the house we rented and stared at the setting sun. "Did you ever think about dying?" Linda said. "I mean, everyone has to die but I just thought about it for me the first time ever. Never hearing or touching or smelling or thinking again. And it gave me the jeebies."

One night I was looking for something to read and I found Linda's Bible from her Sunday School days, her name stamped in silver on the cover. The words sounded pretty: "Walketh not in the counsel of the ungodly. Bringeth forth fruit in season; thy leaf shall not wither."

I looked up. Linda was standing in front of me in a navy blue and white polka-dot dress with a white apron. She held a dustrag. She said, "Sherm, I dust and dust every day, and each night the wind whips up again and blows the dust back in the house. The house must have cracks in it. I can't stand it."

She started bartending three nights a week. The corner tap had a new name, The Why Stop Inn. I stayed home and sat on the porch and enjoyed the smell of the evening, the soil as it cooled that first hour after sunset, the cicadas singing high and electric in the trees. One night, on a whim, I drove to town. Cold air hit me in the face as I opened the door to the bar. "Hey close that," someone yelled. "Make it latch. Keep that hot air out."

Linda was standing in front of the dart board and next to a table with a pitcher of beer and two glasses, and she held a bunch of darts in her hand. Ollie Jensen, who works at the grain co-op, stood behind her with both of his hands on her hips.

She set the darts down and walked toward me in that fast way. She always wore heels. "Sherm," she said, "Ollie's been teaching me to shoot." She kissed me, took off my hat, and hung it up. "Sit down," she said, "and drink some beer."

Ollie Jensen sat on the barstool next to mine. "Does he know about that dead raccoon?" he said.

Linda smiled. "You'll have to ask him."

Ollie said, "She says that on the road to your place there's a dead coon hanging on an electrical pole."

Linda said, "There is, Sherm. He's been hanging there for two weeks and he's going to drop any day. It's across from Dick Falley's place."

I shook my head. "I guess I let my mind drift when I drive," I said.

Ollie said, "I hope he don't let it drift when he's doing something else." He slid off his stool and walked around the corner of the bar and put his arms around Linda.

She said, "Sit down, Ollie." She pushed him away and poured another beer. I told Linda I'd see her in a little bit and I left. I slowed down as I passed the Falley place and something dark and small was hanging from the top of a pole across the road and swaying in the night breeze. At home I sat on the porch with the Bible. "Why do the heathen rage," I read, "and imagine a vain thing?"

When the 4th of July was just around the corner I told Linda I'd like to go Bartlesville for the weekend and stay at a motel and eat in a restaurant. "Just the two of us," I said. But there was a dance and she had to bartend on the sidewalk and she was going in early in the pickup and I was supposed to come by later in the car.

The sun rose high and gold. Steam hovered over the fields. "See you later, Sherm," Linda said. And, the screen door slammed. I read the paper, then looked through it again for news I'd missed: who'd lost the most weight at T.O.P.S., Area Deaths. I showered, put on a short-sleeved shirt and my best hat, and drove to town.

Linda was standing in front of the stage when I got there. Ollie Jensen was there, Arleen Sanders, and the owner of The Why Stop Inn. Linda stood with all of her weight on one leg, on one high-heeled white patent leather sandal, with her arms folded, and she was chewing on her lower lip.

I looked in the same direction she was looking. Tom Horn, a drummer from Pratt, was standing with his hands on his hips, drumsticks sticking out of his back pocket, a cigarette hanging from his mouth. The expression on his face was unpleasant to me.

Then a boy asked Linda to dance. She danced, and she danced with Ollie and the owner of The Why Stop Inn. I drank beer and everyone looked hot. That band finished and came down from the stage and Tom Horn walked over. Linda smiled, then left to pour beer. He followed her and sat at the plank-and-sawhorse bar, staring.

Linda tapped me on the shoulder. "Sherm," she said, "I'm going into the street to dance with Tom Horn."

I went to the park to play horseshoes. When I came back I couldn't find Linda. "Have you seen her?" I asked. No one had. And I found her on a side street, sitting with Tom on the tailgate of our pickup. I said, "We're going home now."

She said, "But I'm supposed to bartend."

I said, "Either you're coming or you're not." I walked away.

She started to follow me, and Tom Horn grabbed her by the belt and jerked her toward him and caught her in his arms. She turned her face to his and laughed. "Sherm," she said, over Tom's shoulder, "wait." I went back to the street and drank whiskey in my beer and danced with Arleen Sanders.

I looked up and saw Linda and Tom Horn.

Linda met my eyes once, then never looked at me again. I watched her bobbing and swaying. I watched her light blue shorts bob and sway in that crowd, and her navy blue sleeveless top was damp and sticking to her sides, and her hair was curly right at the temples. Tom Horn's hand rested in the curve of her back.

Arleen said, "Just ignore them."

A man on stage said, "We'd like to dedicate this song to the pretty ladies of Cherryvale."

I walked over and pushed Tom out of the way. "Whore," I said to Linda, "don't come home."

And I went inside The Why Stop Inn where it was cool and I drank until closing time. Then I went home. I found Linda on the way, on the highway, standing next to our stalled pickup. "I hit a coyote," she said. Parts of it were hanging off the grill: flesh, and pieces of fur. "We'll leave the truck here," I said. We drove home in the car and I gave her my handkerchief because she was crying.

She said she was going to take a bath.

She stood in front of me in a yellow kimono, sipping lemonade through a straw, and she said would I please take a bath with her. She'd draped a rose-colored scarf over the lampshade to make the room dark and she was brushing her hair. She unhooked my pants. She cupped my parts in her hand and laid her face against them. She rubbed her cheek against them and said, "Please, Sherm."

I said, "I'm tired." I went outside and sat in the rocker. I stared at the sky and in a little while I opened the Bible. "All the night I make my bed to swim," I read. "The harried ones cry out. Make no tarrying, O my God."

I fell asleep.

I was in a snow-covered national park, hunting. As the dream continued, I was not a hunter but one of those scientists who protect the animal from people who want its horn or pelt, or the oil from its secret gland. And I was sitting near a stream and in the distance I heard voices, people coming to get it.

"The coon fell off the pole," Linda said. I woke up.

And I thought I should walk in there and lift her out of the tub and carry her somewhere and make love to her, a red candle burning by us, her long wet hair hanging down and wrapping around me. I also thought that men would never quit looking at her and she would always look back and it was only a matter of time before she left. I went into the bathroom to tell her this.

She was sunk under the water, her eyes closed, lips parted.

Her hair floated on the surface in mahogany-colored whorls and her breasts were high and white. I bent down, lifted her up, and breathed into her.

Her eyes fluttered open and she described this dream: "I was in these green woods and I was going to lay in a pool and you woke me. I'm going back there."

I said, "What's in the green woods?"

She didn't answer.

The coroner said afterwards she couldn't have spoken at all except in my imagination, my state of shock. But that's what I remember, also that the scarf she'd draped over the lampshade started to smoke and I pulled it away and turned the lamp off. And when I'd turned off every light in the house, I went back into the bathroom and lifted her up out of the water and carried her away. Her hair hung like seaweed over my arms and water dripped on the floor as I carried her away.

They asked me for a picture they could put in the paper and I sorted through many: Linda as a child, Linda and Sammy standing next to their bikes, Linda holding a seashell, Linda in a plaid blouse and tight bluejeans, standing next to a tractor. Finally, I chose a photo of her taken on the day she went with her high-school class to Wichita to see the refinery. Her arms linked to other arms, her shoulders one set in many, machinery lumbering behind her, she stands alone, a flourish, a cipher. She was buried in a white dress with seed pearls and I helped the undertaker arrange its long folds in the casket. I was wearing a black suit, the only suit I own, and as they lowered her into the ground I looked up and saw the water tower, pale blue and nearly invisible against the sky. The letters had faded. "Many that sleep in dust shall awake," the minister read. It seemed, for a minute, that I had climbed that tower and painted Linda's name, that refrain: On My Mind.

A Pious Wish

I have talent. People said as much when I was the Bow-bells Rodeo Queen and sat on my horse, waving the lithe-wristed beauty queen wave, flicking treats at the youngsters. It's true that I seem to have come down in the world now compared to how I was then, bedecked: satin fringe, a plume in my hat, silver spurs on my feet. Never, the man from the Chamber of Commerce said, in the history of the Bowbells Rodeo had the queen spent so much on clothes. Covetousness is my downfall. ("God forbids also the desire which will move us to get our neighbor's chattel and dunnage, for when lust hath conceived it beareth sin." I memorized that once. It didn't take.) Nevertheless, the high point for me was singing "The Star-Spangled Banner" before the rodeo began and, in particular, the verse I composed myself. Since then I've taken to poems:

> Now I lay me down to see
> if what was true in the past
> is also true now: he loves others better.
> His face, as hard to read as the sky, begs me to stay certain
> I am his best bird, every sigh,
> desire, and hair on my head, numbered. Excuses
> for arbitrary abuse. I walk his line,
> pray about dying. Will I,
> before I sleep?

From that, you'd think I'd been consistently hapless in love but I hadn't. I'd been seduced and deserted, but each time, no matter what might have happened above or below it, my heart stayed staunch. "You haven't met the right man yet," a weathered, painted-up woman I met on a bus said. And the next thing I knew James Dean Wheatley had cracked my egg. All other men ruined forever for me now, I should have said. I did, but it was too late. I gave him my love, sealed in a box, and he didn't give it back. He left it lying on a roadhouse barstool as he followed another farmer's daughter home some coal-dark night, his prong quivering in front of him like a metal detector at a gold site. Unscathedness: that's the quality he locates in a woman those last and potent moments before he believes himself stricken, taken by force into love.

I met him when I was staying at the Catalina Motel, which is of course nowhere near Catalina, being in Louisiana and on the edge of the highway, a two-story, cinder-block building painted aqua. It was a summer evening, warm and turning chilly. I was walking down the street in my white-embossed-roses-on-white sundress which was seven years old at the time and holding up well, looking perhaps more dramatic for its deterioration. I was broke. And James Dean Wheatley leaned out the window of a drive-through liquor store and yelled, "I'm captive. Unchain me." I smiled and continued down the road to the store for cigarettes but made a point of returning by the same route. He came out front then, leaving a customer fuming and stalled in the drive-through, and we made a date for ten o'clock after the liquor store closed.

Making a long story short here, my cash savings dwindled and I professed, unseriously, to look for work in order to keep my room at the Catalina. And, after I'd scanned the want ads for one or two days as James and I sat eating breakfast, stating my misgivings as I did, James asked me to live with him in his blue, run-down house in the middle of the city. But we were evicted for a number of reasons beginning with, first, the fact that Pam, our Doberman pinscher, suffered a panic attack during the 4th of July fireworks display and ate the back door, escaping to terrorize the neighbor's children. Next, someone called the landlord to say I shouted too loud for the summer, windows and doors being open and all and me being either orgasmic or mad at James. And last, James grew agitated himself one night, crossing the street with a baseball bat and running it up and down the picket fence like a hammer against a xylophone, yelling: "Respect! Does it even exist? Who made that up?" The people in question were having a party with soft music and Chinese lanterns in the yard.

And that's how we came to live in the basement apartment in the house on Tilly Street, a fancy street though the apartment itself by no strain of poetic impulse fits that description. "Anyway, please," I said to James when we viewed it, because I pictured myself there, mingling with upper-crust people, developing a reputation as a local poet in flowing dresses, serving tea and biscuits in the afternoon. And I had an intimation that I might get a job after all and infuse my wardrobe and collection of semiprecious jewelry and buy James clothes too. In particular, I saw him in a tie. But James said he wouldn't feel like himself on Tilly Street and he worried about the old man who owned the house and lived upstairs. He felt—and maybe rightly so, it turned out, as several pieces of otherwise small trouble fused together and burned in a straight line toward the end of this run of luck—that the old man was crazy.

"But not," I said, convincing James to move there, "in a dangerous way."

So I put the most attractive of the home furnishings we'd accumulated in three months on top in the cardboard boxes I'd packed, loaded them in the truck, and drove across town. Unloading, I broke a heel. Pam sat in the cab of the truck, leashed to the steering wheel, and howled. I realized, lugging boxes, that the buttons on the bodice of my dress had popped and the raggy, yellowed slip I was wearing on account of it being moving day was revealed. (Never Bleach Lingerie, Hugs Heloise. Life's pressing question is not whether falling trees make sounds in the woods at night, but: why is advice available only too late?) Well, the woman who lives in the house next door stood on her porch in a gray dress, tailored, her hair upswept, arms folded, like a honcho, I thought, high-class, a person who'd believe books about etiquette, proper use of forks and spoons. I set the crate I was carrying down, blotted my face, and said, "Heat excruciates me. I'm Candy Fae Caine Holub. Who are you?"

She said, "Millicent Coals."

James called her Millificent almost from the start, not realizing, kowtowing and scraping as he did, that he'd got it wrong. She liked it; she liked James. That's because, I suppose, her old man's name was Stanley and he played violin and got sick when he thought about eating fish. Now a lot of people feel that way about fish, but for me, and Millicent, concerning Stanley, logic somehow connects the fact that he once almost choked trying to swallow a piece of torsk to the first fact that, when he looks in the mirror, he must realize he looks like a fish. It's not appetizing, not Stanley, not the memory of him spitting in his wine glass, Millicent enjoying the spectacle, James jumping up, the linen napkin dangling from his belt as he wrapped his arms around Stanley and heaved, successfully executing the Heimlich Remover.

I got to know them by dropping in, my hair tied back with a ribbon, and saying: "I see you have a garden and I was just preparing lunch and began to pine for a cucumber." Millicent is one of those women who, though not creative herself, knows folks who are and tends to feed them and give them money. On this particular day I met Dew Cooper and Seymoura Boexx, Dew an artist who pastes things on canvas (mice bones, pencil shavings, ground crystal, pieces of rubber), and Seymoura his long-in-the-face girl-friend. Dew and Seymoura were sitting in the wicker glider on the porch and Stanley sat across from them, holding Seymoura's bare feet in his lap. Seymoura is tall, thin, young, hook-nosed; she was wearing black, shiny pants and I wanted a pair for myself so bad

I felt short-winded. She said, "I want to do something useful with my life, or beautiful." Dew laughed and the sound reminded me of Pam in unison with the noon whistle: lone–some. Seymoura sighed and buried her feet deep in the valley of Stanley's lap.

Millicent spoke and I noticed her way of exhaling on particular words and making them seem like the source of pain. I never got her pegged. Anyway, she said, "JOIN us for a MINT JULEP."

I sat down.

She poured me a drink and said, "As I was saying, ROMANCE is a FICTION."

I tried to decipher that by reversing it: fiction is a romance. And I had a vision: a bare-shouldered, agitated woman on a high wire, quelled in the end by a homely man, stripped, turned handsome.

She said, "What's important is ALLIANCE . . . SOLIDARITY."

Dew said, "Good sex."

I picked a piece of mint off my tongue. "One lover always feels smothered," I said, "while the other one wastes away. And if it feels like that all the time it's infatuation, but if you take turns feeling bad it's love."

Dew smiled.

Millicent said, "This is CANDACE, my neighbor."

I said, "Candy."

Millicent said, "CANDACE is a name with dignity, but CANDY makes you seem trussed-up, ready to eat, NEGLIGIBLE, a snack for MEN."

I understood that right-thinking was at stake.

But the rules seemed unparallel.

I said, "I knew a man in North Dakota who had business cards printed saying he'd eat women because most men there don't. And he always had a date. I don't see what's undignified about that."

Millicent said, "I meant it in the ABSTRACT sense."

I stored that thought away to dwell on.

"Well," I said, "that's fodder for a different horse." And I looked at my hands, thinking, as I do, that the row to hoe since I left Bowbells is long and the things that used to please me (eating, some fucking, and spending money) were ever turning up as loathsome, taboo. Was I supposed to leave it off? I wondered: Oral Sex, along with meat, palm nut oil? Also, I wondered: what did morals have to do with good manners and which did I lack?

Seymoura said, "I have to leave now."

Stanley said, "It's time for me to practice my violin."

Millicent said, "When you come back I have BOOKS I want to lend you."

"Great," I said. "Biography is my favorite."

(I like romance.)

She never even fetched me that cucumber.

MILLICENT'S JOURNAL:

As Candace came up our sidewalk in that frock, a pale bow wound around her black hair, her skin vermillion and cream, her demeanor at once frail and disquietingly robust, I considered how trouble is big, ancient, issued forth from genes, not a result of experience alone. In my travels, in Africa, I watched a lion beat his cub as though to implant pain, a lesson, and the lioness rushed in with ministrations, her tongue lapping the cub as though to say: the price of freedom is asylum. And I despair of changing the world but my desire to do it is what I have, not art, not love. And so, when Candace protested my complaint against the diminution of her name, my heart cracked as though my lover had waved good-bye. My psychiatrist once said that, like the lioness who perpetuates dependency, I must leave off ministrations and succor too; yet, in spite of that, because of it, I saw through her garish clothes, the ruse, through the fact of her unfolding like a flower under the gaze of men, that Candace is gifted, inducing new conclusion from old experience. And she folds back up again as though the day were chilly. I want to save her and feel that, in the act of salvage, my longing for a mended world will convert to substance, my desire to ice . . .

Anyway, I went back to our apartment, which was empty except for Pam because James was at the liquor store. And I thought that wanting good taste was nothing compared to having it, like Millicent, having soaked in it in her mother's belly and from the time she burst out continuing to get: an aura, transportable. I, on the other hand, always try someone else's taste on, borrow a cup of it, and, venturing forth, reveal myself: Candy Fae Caine. I sat on the prickly sofa and stared at the wallpaper with the splotchy silver stars and tried to have uplifting thoughts. I remembered Miss Rhodie, my high school teacher, who said: Poetry is Religion. That took. Well, I changed into my sienna-colored dress, slid turquoise and agate jewelry up my arms, and read one of my own poems out loud:

Hungry
enough, sometimes I say
to men: we eat first, talk later.
Lovemaking is good or bad. I don't
take advice, my pranks being nobody's business, but once
I got a day job and settled. Then, in the night,
in my apartment, the black phone shivered
and rang: I think about you, a whisper said.
I recognized the voice and battened down my hatch hard.
I sought a motto: Live to Die.
The End is Soon. No one Leaves or Enters. Nothing
Washes
Away.

But I didn't like it now, I decided, thinking that if it did show up in a book people would say it was me, a slut, my black phone shaking and sending out messages and those facts my fault.

That was the advice I'd gotten so far.

For instance, James said: "Shouldn't you make things up? Isn't that the point?" I'd read him my poem about falling asleep in a high-dollar hotel lobby and waking up with my lipstick smeared on the cushions and the doorman nearby, glowering. It ends with the generalization that life is one long flight out of coops. James also says, when I show him my poems at night: "How interesting." Or: "Let's lift up your nightgown and look at your legs."

That's what I was thinking when someone knocked on the door. It was the landlord.

I call him that, though the whole time we lived in that basement apartment he never asked for rent, a fact that caused James some guilt and even I see his point, Luther's Catechism saying for instance that we shouldn't get our neighbor's goods by false ware or deals. But I don't waste money. I told James I'd pay the rent, a prevarication I grant, but only because he harped. Anyway, I made two cups of Earl Grey tea, fetched a box of Lorna Doones, and asked the landlord in, thinking, as he sat there sipping and wiping crumbs off his lips, that he was about to bring the subject of back-rent up. Instead, he said, "I was buying a can of motor oil and I met a woman I want to ask to be my wife, and I was wondering if you'd invite her here to introduce me?"

It turns out he'd met a woman at a gas station down the street.

"You mean like a blind date?" I said.

He nodded.

I said, "Well, I can't because I don't know her and it'd seem outlandish." And I told him about a woman from the East who'd moved to Bowbells and went to VFW halls and tried to get the local women to dance with her, saying it was done all the time where she came from because men don't dance there, and most men in North Dakota don't either and it'd seemed like a solution, but the idea was off-putting to the locals, many of whom were cool even to me just because I danced with her once. I wasn't sure why I was telling the landlord this, his name is Mason Ball, or if it was linked to what he'd asked or my predicament. "Get my drift?" I said.

He said, "You're saying I should ask someone to marry me who I know."

"Right," I said. And I mentioned that the bedroom window was swollen shut and how I'd developed a fear of sleeping in that low room with no outlet. I recalled, also, a magazine article I'd read that said people who were afraid of small spaces used sex the way other folks use drugs, to escape Fear of Death. For me it was the opposite, I used it to escape boringness, the ordinary, boredom. "Can you fix it?" I said to the landlord, meaning the window. I handed him tools. I picked up my poems to read them again and, just as I was launching into one, he yelled from the bedroom, wrenching the window open, "Love is a clever monkey."

That's what I thought he said. Crack-brained, I decided, but also, my back to him, considering meanwhile how he had blue, kind eyes, that it wasn't as though I'd never spent time with crazy people, and I thought particularly about my uncle whose penchant it was to walk downtown and ask salesgirls to help him buy underwear and how my mother used to make me go with him so I could talk him into coming home. I mentioned that to Mason Ball too.

The telephone rang and I picked it up. "Hello, James," I said. Time weighs heavy on his hands on the day shift at the liquor store.

He said, "What's a six-letter word meaning to adhere and separate?"

"Cleave," I said.

The landlord said, "Love springs up as the fleshpots decay."

James said, "Who's there?"

I hung up.

The landlord stood in the doorway then and banged his knuckles against the frame. I thought, first, how he wasn't old enough to be my father who I've searched for since he left, before

I was born. He was wearing a hat, both my father in the one photo I have and Mason Ball. All men look cute in hats, their ebbing hairlines unrevealed; I am drawn, though, as a canoe to the edge of waterfalls, to truly bald men, their shining pates seeming to me superior, exotic compared to the merely human *haired* head, or *semihaired*. And Mason Ball stuck his tongue out as if to show me he was sucking on a red-and-white peppermint. "Good-bye," he said. "Thank you for your advice. We have a lot in common."

I shut the door and thought about that.

There was another knock and I figured it was the landlord returning, but it was Dew Cooper in a pair of tight black pants (Seymoura's? I wondered), a black T-shirt, a pair of red canvas high-tops with silver stripes and laces. Dew is different from anyone, his black hair buzz-cut so short it has nap, like velvet, his eyelashes curving up and forward like points of spidery lace. I remember what Miss Rhodie said about the time she was in California and heard Allen Ginsberg read poems and tried to seduce him later: "His mouth was red and full like a sex organ." Dew's was like that. To answer the other question: how urged toward him was I? Another article I read said nymphomaniacs don't make love because they like it but because they don't like it enough.

He'd brought along a packet of cocaine. I showed him my poems, beginning with the one about being hungry and having sex because of it and the telephone ringing. "It needs a label to constellate its parts," he said. And he asked me if I was hungry, if I needed to go somewhere for lunch; I said no. He said, "I give my paintings names like 'Blue Monday' or 'The Writing on the Wall,' and that way endow the fragments in them with a reason to coexist."

"I mean to call this poem 'Tattoo' for the same reason," I said.

He said, "Some magazine will go for it—rural, affirmative, dark-image, woodsy, surreal." He told me about one named *Raccoon* in Memphis, Tennessee, which advertises itself as needing poems that express the deep-root desire to be written, no intellectual tidbits.

I said, "It's not a nature poem."

He said, "I like my despair aestheticized." And he flung the sheaf of papers across the room.

I thought: Despair?

Aestheticized?

I'd have to look it up. One of my favorite things, besides *Heloise's Book of Household Hints* and the Concordance in the Bible where you find words to trace them to meaningful verses (i.e., Moon, idolatrously worshipped, Deut. 17:3 . . .), is the dictionary.

Anyway, Dew kneeled down, slid my shoe off, put my foot in his mouth, and sucked my toes. I suppose he thought I'd never had that done, being rural and all, but he was wrong. And I remembered, oddly, considering it was Dew kneeling in front of me, and me, a human, sitting on that footstool and getting my toes sucked, that it was common for men to fantasize about having sex with extraterrestrials, the point being to reduce to normal the extraordinary by interbreeding. I mean this in the *abstract* sense.

Dew said, "Delectable, Candy. By no means negligible."

I shut my eyes.

"Flee and avoid opportunity for lust" was the phrase that came to mind.

Mottos never usually flash on my screen when I make love and I like that, my head empty and me drawing pictures. James says, about the faraway look in my eyes, "You wish I was taller, smarter, more handsome." I say, "I am thinking about breezes, James, blue horses, the babbling and powerful sky." Well, my mother warned me sex would be fizzled-out and not to look forward to it. She was taking a bath at the time, drinking vodka, her body lobbing in the water. I spent my first womanly years trying to prove that wrong. Miss Rhodie said sex was like this: "A door opening like a door and closing like a mountain." That came back to me once as I lay on a hard-tiled floor, a bulky lover whose name I don't remember washed over above me by a tide of ideas that left me dry. "You know what I mean," he said. I didn't. And I thought, cocaine burning in my head, Dew's ministrations for me a nuisance like a bottle fly buzzing against glass, that it was the mention of Oral Sex, earlier, on Millicent's porch, that had sent him scurrying like a drooling Pavlov rat. I stared up at the open window, its sad rag of flapping curtain. "Relax, Candy," Dew said, "you're not at the dentist."

I heard James rattling the back door I'd had the foresight to lock.

Dew stopped.

James yelled. "Candy. Candy."

Dew said, "Of all the impediments I'd considered, this wasn't one."

MILLICENT'S JOURNAL:

I had a teacher, in private school, in my variegated past, who would write on the board "Art is . . ." and we'd answer, by rote, ". . . ordered. The author's hand, not God, controls it." Yet there are coincidences so canny no author or deity (except Dionysus, perhaps, that sadistic fag) would plant. I refer to the conglomeration of trouble, the chaff-triggered sequence of grief, inconvenience, events like spurs growing large and gathering, meanwhile, speed. I try to understand why, when recovery is imminent, I've grown attached again to the notion of tutelage: Candace requiring it this time, and me, as always, wise as sage. (What is the Rorschach test anyway but an explication of vision?) I think: Candace, her unruly hair restrained, knocking, asking, can I spare produce from my garden, as though, like the impoverished princess in fables, she'd fail without it. I grow intoxicated by this, and then (oh my poisoned heart) see from my window, rising like smoke out of what I know to be Candace's bedroom window, Dew Cooper, naked, that bastard, dragging his clothes behind him, jumping in them again under the lilac trees and fleeing, minus one shoe. Next I see that handsome man, James (to whom, nonetheless, I can never imagine myself speaking), his muscles taut as he circles the house, rattling its doors, windows: Let

me in. Even his posture says that. I picture Candace inside,
hounded for the wrong reason, Sex, and I yield: I'll teach her,
I decide, to molt, ameliorate, fly . . .

Well, I considered later, when I found myself in a peck of
trouble, that hanging up the phone when James had said, spooked,
green-eyed, "Who's there with you?" was a cry for help, my Freud-
ian half-slip, wishful thinking: James come home and help me
resist the temptation to adulterate, please. But I doubted it, considering it was Mason Ball the landlord with me and that I hung
up because James gets on my nerves when he implies that I cheat
with outlandish candidates, the carry-out boy at the grocery store,
for instance. Once, being preoccupied with the concept of lust in
my heart, he asked if I'd thought about having sex with anyone
but him and, feeling contrary, I batted my eyelashes and said,
"Yes, Pam. And I guess that makes me a lesbian."

Pam was a source of trouble anyway, flexing her eyebrow muscles, whining, thumping her tail as she gazed up at the window
Dew had crawled through—and after I'd spent fifteen minutes
convincing James I was napping naked in the middle of the day
because the excruciating Louisiana heat had made me vaporous,
weak. "Well, what is it, Pam?" James said. And she let out one of
those whines that sounds like a yawn and dragged from under the
bed Dew's last trace, a shoe I hadn't located in time to throw out
the window with the rest of his clothes. James held it by its lace,
dangling, as though he'd get contaminated, and frowned.

I said, "Pam, you ratting, tattling bitch . . ."

James said, "What?"

I said, "That was one of your birthday gifts."

He stared at the shoe (he wears 14EE, a rare size) and my plan
had been to buy time anyway, to postpone convulsions of strain
or shock until what I think of as James's natural amnesia set in.

Someone knocked on the door and James dropped the shoe on
the floor.

If I would have had my wits with me—had they not flown out the window towards some place occupied by creatures somewhat like humans but more like soap opera characters in that their lives are accentuated with tension, withheld information ("Will Dew return to the scene and debase Candy in front of her stolid lover, James?")—I would have picked the shoe up and got rid of it.

But I was too nervous to think like that.

I thought instead: What a relief. Because, when James opened the door, it was the landlord.

He walked in carrying a cellophane bag of those mints he always sucks on, a housecoat, an umbrella, also one of those pens you get in your stocking at Christmas that looks like a barbershop pole bent over or, more certainly, a candy cane. Everything, the mints, the housecoat, and so on, and of course the pen designed to look like my name, was red-and-white striped.

He said, "These items remind me of you."

I said thank you, but that I'd kept the last name of my ex-husband Don Holub who I was married to for only three weeks in order to dilute that effect—my name always putting people in mind of Christmas.

Mason said, "What name?"

I said, "Candy Fae Caine and, recently, Holub."

"Oh," he said. "Well, I had no idea."

I took the gifts out of his arms then and acted happy, remembering my Aunt Lana who complains about presents people give her. "I have one of these," she says, or "I saw this at the Wal-Mart and I like the other color better." Meanwhile, James looked bewildered. It used to be easy to think of him as having chosen the strong, silent personality because he wasn't smart, liable to glitch when he heard or saw something new. But now he's a puzzle, a question, the fish that swam away having swallowed and not relinquished me, the bait. I'm seduced by legends. James, let me recall this, never drew attention to other people's bad habits. ("We may not belie our neighbor but defend him and put the best construction on everything.") And that's why he's hard to spot, like a scrap of wallpaper cut out and hung in its place in the pattern.

The landlord left and I smiled. I didn't consider the shoe. "I do need an umbrella," I told James, "but the housecoat is a travesty."

And at that moment, like an odometer clicking to 100,000, James stopped being my lover and I became his.

My first time.

James, the lovee.

His first, second, or three-hundred-and-forty-fifth time, I have no idea.

I noticed the change later and traced it back: the shell (James smitten by and doting on me) cracked open to reveal its core (James enraged); the PAST, in which I was an angel who fell because of hard luck, cracked open to reveal the PRESENT, in which I was a whore, indiscriminate, in which, moreover, James pounded his chest and yelled he wouldn't abide hijinks and no longer found attractive a high IQ or sense of adventure if the person who had those things told complex lies on short notice to save her hide or—this was worse, he thought—make the people she told them to look ridiculous. His face twisted and red, he picked up the umbrella Mason Ball gave me and smashed every lamp in the house.

Then, taking a breather, he said, "I recognize the smell of sex."

That's how I got caught: smell.

Like the man in North Dakota with the business cards about Oral Sex whose wife picked him up from work, leaned over to kiss him, inhaled deep, and—I watched from the parking lot—slapped him hard.

James smashed the first window.

I watched: one, two, three, the succession. Glass tinkling like bells.

He said, "I think of you diddling that codger for rent and lose my senses more."

I seized on that. If I could find a way, I thought, to prove, regarding Mason Ball at least, that I was innocent, the past might stay linked to the present and I'd have love and eat it too; I'd relish in, and lavish on James, getting and giving for the first time in the history of it, love.

James knocked all the windows out, even the one in the bedroom, newly opened and latched to the ceiling, that Dew had crawled through.

He mopped his brow. His face, agonized, noble, reminded me of a documentary I'd seen called *Faces of Victory*, about soldiers, athletes, people who've won. I also remembered a stallion I'd seen locked up, famed, murderous ("This horse caused the deaths of three men who tried to break him . . ."), his muscles clenching and unclenching beneath his shiny black coat, blue in the bleaching, toxic sun.

James said, "Read poetry out loud, Candy."

I was surprised, worried, remembering the night when, sick of it, James got drunk, locked himself in the pantry, and called me Miss Poem.

But he was waving the umbrella, a gesture I saw as dangerous. So I recited:

> If I start trying now . . .

I began,

> lay my reservations down and say I want it,
> and don't get it, no one will call it Fear (of Love),
> the goblin in the closet keeping me remote.

I saw myself as charmed, changing straw to gold, vying for the position of king's lover, not ordinary, not the girl from the outlands with pretty hair for whom, just the same, straw remains straw and the future grows bleak.

> My pulse gnarled . . . ,

I said,

> my body hot, but the rest of me cold:
> my heart, never attacked. Love comes,
> sits on my chest, blows in my face. I see him and think
> I should make a record how he got there.
> Who will call that anything but nerves, the buzzsaws?
> Oh, I'd react: a pulmonary squeal, my breath
> cluttering up the air. I'd get over this
> brick cliff or hole—Love—too,

I stopped to see if James were watching. He wasn't.
I finished,

> . . . eyes closed.

My power was gone. Would its absence make James's heart
strong?

When it had worked, it was under his skin, sending him into
rages or elaborate lies by which he tried to seem not bothered
by poems, not, as he'd put it himself, as though the person who
wrote them had poison ivy and was doing her best to make sure
he got it too. Now my poems had only the effect he used to wish
they had: making him sleepy like a productive milk cow in a stall
with Brahms piped in.

"Read another one," he said.

That's when Millicent knocked on the door and stepped inside,
carefully over the broken shards of glass swirled like mosaic. She
was wearing a cape, carrying a basket of cucumbers, zucchini,
tomatoes, yellow crooknecks. "I brought you these," she said, "and
an INVITATION. CANDACE, I'd like you to come over this afternoon and talk about ISSUES of WOMANHOOD, and BOOKS
and . . ."

She breathed deeply and faced James.

". . . I don't want to leave YOU out. Please join us, my LOVER
Stanley and ME, and Candace of course, this evening, for dinner."

I started to say, "James doesn't like to eat dinner anywhere but

here because casseroles are his favorite dish, my recipes especially."

This had been true in the past.

But, before I could, James answered, like a husband, like someone an ordinary woman would trust, "Stanley is the one who
mows your lawn, the guy who carries the violin case and drives
a Volvo, right? We'd be delighted." As though he, James, mowed
lawns, played violins, had anything at all to do with life as it was
on Tilly Street.

I'd started to pick up the larger pieces of glass and put them
in a trashbasket. What did Millicent think of the evidence, visible
everywhere and sharp-edged, of the last half-hour's fight? "I'll see
you in an HOUR," she said to me. "And . . ." She looked at James
again and blushed, the color of her cape, red. "YOU, this evening.
Meanwhile, I'm off to my ARTS COUNCIL meeting."

"Arts council," I said flatly. I had a glass sliver in my thumb.
I felt unequal to conversation about things I didn't understand;
my verve, gone. The cure for that was drunkenness, life baptized
by no-life and the long climb back, gratitude for life restored, its
unblinkingness.

James said, "Arts council, how interesting."

The same man to whom, months earlier, I'd described what
a poetry reading was and he said: "Poultry reading?" As though
chickens, not poems, were the objects of interest and you picked
them up in candle-lit rooms and told the future from crags in
their feet.

It might have been a joke.

Millicent said, "We determine which projects are most worthy
to be funded by state monies."

Monies, I thought.

James said, "I'll be darned."

Millicent left then and I cleaned the apartment while James
stood by the window which faced the street, and worried me
again; he read my poems, some out loud, gesturing meanwhile as

if he were auditioning, others in a monotone for whom, I suppose, he was the audience.

"Great," he said. "Poetry is my favorite."

And he pointed out the window and said: "My hell."

I stopped sweeping and looked up.

Stanley was getting out of a car wearing swimming trunks, carrying a violin case, a jungle-print beach towel, a bottle of liquor. Seymoura, Dew Cooper's lover, it seemed, was naked behind the wheel.

I figured it out. "She's wearing a strapless swimsuit," I said.

She put our minds to rest then by getting out of the car in a bandeau-style, two-piece black suit, chasing Stanley to the porch, flinging her long, flexible arms around him, and kissing him hard. She drove away, her hair rising like smoke out the window.

I thought how James had said "My hell" as in "My personal hell revisited."

But he'd said it all along, I told myself, ever since I met him, over things as inconsequential as the newspaper not being delivered.

"Funny thing," I said.

James said, "Funny." He picked up my poems, some scattered among glass pieces on the floor, some stacked on the window ledge, some on the couch, the vanity, the bed, and set them on a table in the center of the room, carefully, with a beer can for a paperweight.

MILLICENT'S JOURNAL:
"Things fall apart; the center will not hold." I thought this as I minced vegetables for our feast, though I decided some time ago it was wrong to obsess about tornados and fault lines. My psychiatrist believes the down-spiral of negative projection is reversible: gloomy thoughts must be sent back up their coils to the top. I'm worried since my afternoon with Candace, the session in which I became aware that the violence we have witnessed is a rumbling black cloud, hovering, which may

strike above the table at dinner tonight and fall, lightning's blade. Candace's edge is lost, her contentiousness dulled. I say this because she was easily taught today, resisting no dictum. Obsequiousness might ultimately destroy her, her poetry, rich, piercing, raw, but she must be stripped of trouble-generating clichés.

Teaching is a profession deemed noble, sacrificial, like martyrdom or motherhood if you get paid for it, but if it's chosen like I have chosen it, for love, not money, it's suspect, crank. (Would a good man, not Stanley, cure me?) I said to Candace, read this book. She crossed her legs, chewed her thumb, sighed. "I heard about it," she said, "keeping your man by being sexy, meeting him at the door naked but wearing Saran Wrap. That won't help me." I paused before I realized she'd confused the book I was referring to, Betty Friedan's *The Feminine Mystique,* with that retrogressive tract by Marabel Morgan, *The Total Woman.* I explained the difference: we do not, I said, subscribe to theories which interpret our ability to transmogrify into objects to be penetrated in a variety of ways as the hinge upon which our relations with and confidence in the men we love depend.

"No," she said, "I guess not. Do you have something to drink?"

She had two glasses of Absolut vodka with no ice or garnish while I determined what book would inspirit her. A stack of them sat on the table.

She saw *The Cinderella Complex* and brightened. "I've seen myself like that," she said.

No doubt it is her text, I thought, depicting addiction to crisis, describing the impetus to drive everything, as she'd driven that handsome man James, to a state so extreme glass broke. Still, I admired her calm, remembering my cowardice in the days I used to try to keep Stanley from his affairs with women who no doubt understood him better than I could, his masculine dilemma. I remember, particularly, the night he smashed the Haviland china which had been my mother's, and I drove to a motel and nightmared until morning about the delicately sprigged shards of porcelain on the floor and how they'd never come together again, Humpty-Dumpty's death. I returned home and packed the fragments in a lined box, still housed somewhere in the attic, cobwebbed recesses of memory.

Candace said something strange: "Love is a clever monkey."

I said, gently, of course, "Candace, trouble seems to be your habit."

Rocking back and forth in the chair, slopping the vodka she poured into her glass, she looked up, eyes brilliant and clouded over as stars in the gray sky. "Trouble, my lover," she said, "what a clue."

"Life's indexes," I thought, slipping drunkenly out of my sienna-colored dress to prepare for dinner that night at Millicent's.

"Life's textbooks."

These were Miss Rhodie's phrases of course, her way of describing astrology guides, the Bible, the *Collected Works of Keats*, the *Encyclopedia of Symptoms*, all of which she had lined in a row on the mantel in the living room of her ivy-covered frame house in Bowbells. I was homesick, I thought. Would the catalpa tree be dropping its blossoms, making the fragrant carpet I used to lie down upon as I stared up into the branches, the complex city of birds? ("I do not think that I should ever see a poem as lovely as a tree . . .")

But it was October, not June; however far away North Dakota seemed, it was October everywhere, the season for shutting down.

I made as if to shut down and saw myself in the mirror, hunched over in my slip, turquoise and agate bracelets still on my arms. I slid them off and put on, instead, the red-and-white plastic beaded things Mason Ball had given me only moments earlier, tapping on the back door, whispering, sensing, I guess, that James was jealous. ("Jealousy is an emotion I choose not to feel," Millicent had said, "though not everyone is GIFTED.") Significant, I thought, the red-and-white bracelets; for I no longer saw myself as fit for semiprecious stones, least of all *precious* like Millicent's, her opals and rubies glowing like coals.

James came in the room wearing a tie like the one the hero on "The Wild, Wild West" always wore, and shiny, polished shoes. What a face, I thought, remembering how I'd invested in it, that righteous mouth, when I'd first met him and not yet pegged him as easily gulled; but I had, and in spite of my pious wish to be something besides my natural self, glib and abusive, like a reformed street wino with hooch wafting nearby, I gave up the hope.

"You're not wearing that," James said, meaning my slip.

I said, "James, you told me you wouldn't feel like yourself in a tie."

He said, "No. I told you I didn't need a new tie and you made up the rest."

We went to Millicent's for dinner and the night runs together after that, static on my screen. James taught me to eat artichokes, to strop my teeth against the leaves; he whispered, when my eyes widened at the plate of it set before me, pink and glistening, topped with capers (green spheres that taste like nail-polish remover), that some salmon is supposed to be eaten raw.

Stanley left the room.

Millicent said, as she broke bread, "How provincial, I think, to find NAUSEATING anything outside one's SMALL realm of experience." She elaborated, loud enough for Stanley, in the next room, waiting, to hear: "He was raised in the Midwest where the only fish is catfish; its bloated lips scour the river bottom for TRASH, CARRION. It's an ANALOGY, you see—the community of artists and their lovers, the river bottom, ready for the SUCKING UP, and Stanley the aquatic equivalent of the VULTURE, a SUPREME CATFISH he's confused with every fish he's seen on a plate since and, therefore, fearing self-destruction, reverencing the FLESH of his own species, he refuses to DINE with us NOW." She smiled as she said this, and ladled tarragon cream onto a fillet of torsk.

Stanley came back into the dining room then and proved he was a man, no fish, by chunking off a piece of torsk and swallowing it. You know the rest: how he jumped up from the table, knocked over a Grecian urn, and nearly choked until James saved him.

I saw it all, blurred, as if through murky water, and sipped wine and thought how Millicent's analogy was right, that the power of suggestion had been once and for all proven because Stanley looked walleyed and pasty and, though not like a torsk or salmon, certainly as if he'd gone through evolution by a detour.

He left, squealing wheels.

If I trust my intuition, also the information passed on to me later—that Dew Cooper trashed Stanley's Volvo that night, using a coat hanger to write profanities in the pearl-gray paint, dropping cinder blocks on the hood—then it's safe to say he went straight to Seymoura's. At any rate, a few months later Stanley and Seymoura turned up in the Society and Arts page of the newspaper, holding hands at a fund-raiser for authors called The Writes of Spring.

Next Millicent served liquor in crystal glasses and we watched a TV show about big felines crawling across rocks, snarling, showing their teeth. "RAW," Millicent said, "and so MAGNIFICENT."

James agreed. And he started calling her Millificent, which made me think of a cartoon witch but also of the time I was supposed to say in church, before first communion, "We are buried with Christ by baptism."

And what I said was: "We are buried with crap."

"Is that your OPINION, Candace?" Millicent said.

(I'd said that last part out loud.)

"Jungle cats do remind me of Raquel Welch," I said, perhaps irrelevantly, "or any cheap woman who tries to look like that."

Primal, I meant, and, exempting myself from the label, thought of women who frequent James's liquor store on Friday nights, their hair tangly, sinewy limbs clad in fabric with palm-swatch or animal-skin designs, lower eyelids outlined in black. They buy pink wine. I was thinking of Seymoura too. "You know," I said to James, "how we used to watch and keep track of how many we'd see a night." Leopard-spotting, we'd called it, our best shared joke.

James said, "Hush, Candy." And he and Millicent started to gasp and demonstrate awe, for on the TV screen at that moment were two birds in a ritual of seduction, flying backwards in delicate rhythm, motion slowed, a waltz. And the sound track mewled out something with violins and flutes. "How beautiful," Millicent said.

"Your problem," James said to me, "is that you don't appreciate nature."

Well, I waited all night for climax. The TV droned. James and I went home.

He slept in his underwear, not naked.

I got down on my knees, next to the bed, and said, "James, my heart, an armored thing, but sweet and tender and worth having on the inside." I was thinking of a cactus, I guess; I didn't tone it down, my penchant for words whipping even sincere ideas to froth. ("Impatience is a virtue," an old boyfriend of mine, a chef, had once said, impressed at how fast I peeled garlic.) "Don't leave me alone with this big, vegetable love," I told James, finally.

Or something like that.

He patted me on the head and went to sleep.

I stayed up all night, to the point of dawn when straight lines waver, when walls come apart and the dowels in the stairway banister ripple and bow, a chorus. Cool, wet air blew through the windows, broken open now, letting in all the sense of risk anyone could want; I hated it. I kept watch as the hours bonged by and cleaned house as though it were spring, every crevice and groove my target, using an old toothbrush and an Heloise formula to scour the useless filigree of baseboards, cupboards, furnace grates, anything functional made too complicated by design. When James got up, I laid out freshly ironed clothes and breakfast: sunshiney eggs, red tomato juice, crisp, streaky bacon. He left for work and I stood in the doorway in my red-and-white striped housecoat and waved, Pam at my feet, flapping her thick tail good-bye. At the intersection at the end of the block, James stopped, turned around, and looked at me through the rear window of the truck. Things can be made to blow over, I told myself, even disappear.

MILLICENT'S JOURNAL:

Gone, the two of them, James and Stanley in the same day, like leaves off trees, the difference being that I banished Stanley in my unprecedentedly assertive fashion while Candace, also for the first time in her life, grew mute, begging James, by deed and gesture, to stay. My theory of crisis failed. Crux: n., a singularly critical point which develops as lines of otherwise discrete trouble intersect and—BANG, BANG— make for irrevocable change. But at what moment? Candace had hers, surely, the glass breaking. But why not six months before it, or after, or six minutes, or two days? How does one foretell and hence *avoid* trouble? I watched Candace, at dinner, and later, out my window and through hers, on hands and knees: repentant. And, still, James left. The first eight hours he should have been at work, and was, for some of them, I have details; even when he didn't return that night we thought he was drinking hard, courting another woman, making a point. And so we were left to synthesize hypothetical clues like detectives investigating murder without a corpse. (At least I have Stanley's picture in the paper once in a while, pallor accentuated, proof.) James, on the other hand, became a legend.

Why? When?

Does trouble culminate by repetition, gathering speed each lap? Is it an engine dragging attendant causes behind? What about this clue, a letter?

Dear Millificent,

I owe you this explanation for leaving when we'd grown so close in the last day, peas in a pod. I met a woman, she walked right in the liquor store, Marie, who I hope will be the best of both kinds of women, beautiful on the outside, like Candy who, just the same, disappointed me for her lack of moral content. I hope Marie will be beautiful on the inside too. If things don't work out with her I'm giving up on outside beauty altogether and coming back for you,

Love James.

Is this the gawky sentiment that lurks below that surface, lovely, his face and body? Is it a joke on Candace, me, our affinity for tropes, words, labels? Oh, all that has been attributed to silence in the past: strength, wisdom, modesty. I think, for instance, of Robert Zimmerman—a prophet, or just lucky and stupid. Or Singer in *The Heart Is a Lonely Hunter* who asks: Why do people move their lips at me? What do they want? And renditions of God, fist raised in the air: Stern? Angry? or Confused? (Oh Jesus thinks hard about things all right, he's just nonverbal.)

Farewell, psychiatry.

As I give myself over to this desire to help Candace, I ask myself: how? Having found what I've searched for, talent to cultivate, to expose to sunlight and pour water on: how? Should she write in the great yoked, collared tradition: O Batter Her Heart? Should she be tutored: allusive though disempowered? Or, falling back hard on autobiography, will she run out of steam? Can she avoid trouble, recalling only youthful bouts tranquilly? Does art feed life, or only off of it, a scavenger? And last, will either of us be better at anything, besides the Sunday crossword puzzle perhaps, for having labored at it?

What's it good for, I want to know, finally, if it doesn't bring what it used to, comfort? When Miss Rhodie had said, Poetry is Religion, I took that literally, as opposed to ABSTRACTLY, turning to words for consolation (<L. *religio,* bond between man and the gods). But I didn't have to take Miss Rhodie's advice; I'd been doing it anyway, exaggerating, making things up, writing Bible chapters that suited me better than King James's.

You can't write another verse for "The Star-Spangled Banner."

Why not?

Liar, cheat.

But Millicent makes me aware I've been going at it like a hack. I've put myself under her wing, as under Miss Rhodie's before, and they've begun to look alike to me; ten years from now I'll recall something one of them once taught me but won't be able to say which one it was any more than I'd be able to tell you now whether a yellow house I once lived in on a street named Logan Avenue with rhododendrons next to the driveway was in Tucson or Cincinnati, even though I lived there, I'm sure, for years.

These are things I think about as I sit in the airy basement apartment on Tilly Street and do my homework. In the afternoon, I write poems. Late at night, and in the morning, I read books and report back to Millicent for dinner: we eat good food, talk, and afterwards, for pleasure, play cards—"Loo"—in the parlor. Last night she told me how, when she was an undergraduate, she had a professor who dressed like John Donne, wore his beard like him, spent the whole semester not teaching but reading the poems in a booming voice, and Millicent's infatuation grew until she'd checked out of the library every book by or about John Donne, and a copy of the one portrait of him, in his coffin, in white, swaddling graveyard clothes, hung over her bed.

This could go on forever, Millicent feeding me, no rent necessary for Mason Ball, who loves me and continues to haunt garage sales to bring me red-and-white trifles which I use, consume: a bag of peppermints, for instance, every week. But I remember a piece of my mother's advice, a sentiment, moreover, of which James Dean Wheatley, who is to me what John Donne is to Millicent, would approve: Be beholden to no one, pay your own way.

The source of trouble, I think, the incident I zero down to as having begun this irrevocable, claptrap mess, was making love to Dew Cooper when the urge for him wasn't irresistible, as it sometimes has been in my past, a hurricane whirling toward an abyss. Why did I sleep with him? A democratic impulse, I think: why should he, I'd wondered, be deprived of sex with me, it being no fault of his that he looks like an effete, homosexual satyr and doesn't get laid anyway except by that underfed Seymoura, and who was I to keep him from one shot at a healthy, strapping woman?

That was my logic.

If I had it to do over, of course, I'd skip Dew and keep James because I miss him and he's in love with a girl named Marie now who, Millicent tells me, he met in a bar or some place like that.

I picture them swirling together to the lyrics of a sad, lilting song: Sometimes it's hard . . .

. . . giving all your love to just one man.

Someone to cling to when nights

are Cold

. . . and Lonely.

The last piece of news is that my poetic impulse wanes. Millicent notices too, though she pretends not to: Be still it will come again, she says, quoting Theodore Roethke to make it so. But even read out loud in front of the mirror, my poems have nothing going for them in the way they used to. I put on all the different colored dresses I own, though that's mostly red now, and nothing happens. On one occasion, I started to read a stanza I'd begun

about James, and Pam sobbed, howled, rubbed her nose against
the door.

What is it, I asked, the poem?

A good man
came. And I laid down,
every time after crawling away to fetch my chemise,
feeling sweet,
thinking of him above me like weeds, dusty and whispering
he could not bear
to let me go.
The welding together hurt
and relieved me but . . .

There was a knock at the door. My heart thumped. James, I prayed,
returning.

But it was Dew Cooper with Chinese food and he insisted we
eat. "We eat first, talk later," he said. Then he noticed the condition
of the apartment, its lights punched out, the wide-open windows.
It was as though his stiff, bristly hairs stood up straighter and his
eyebrows arched. "What happened?" he asked, breathing hard. At
that moment, someone else knocked on the door and Dew fled,
like before, but fully clothed this time, out the window.

Pam and I stared after him.

I answered the door.

It was Mason Ball with a red-and-white lawn chair with alu-
minum rockers.

"For the front porch," he said. He had one for himself too. I had
a dream, recently, in which Mason Ball took off the gardening hat
he always wears and underneath it was a gloriously bald head,
emanating, believe it, rays of light. I watched as he moved from
room to room, beams ferreting out the corners, refracting as they
shone across right angles, walls, ceilings. And he put the hat back
on and said, "Honey, it's always right here if you need it." I woke up

up then and thought about going upstairs to get in bed with him, not for sex, understand, but in the way I might have if I'd had a father when I was a little girl and frightened.

"That's what the Heavenly Father's for," a preacher once said.

And Mason Ball said, "Let's bask in last yellow pools of light."

So we set the striped chairs on the front porch and savored what was left of the season for, though in Louisiana there is no winter in the northern sense of the word, beauty, belief in possibility, fades away.

I considered the days ahead, my options: one, tracking James down; two, slapping Marie senseless, saying, You ain't woman enough; three, reminding James of the PAST, you used to love *me*.

And the FUTURE, my pleasure in it, began:

I enter a profession, hairdressing, where gossip and lies are part of the day, and I don't subject James to them at night anymore, metered, on paper, when he'd rather make love; I worm my way back to his muscled heart. Or I stay here, among books, oily food, gewgaws. Or I return to North Dakota, to Miss Rhodie, the Chamber of Commerce, my mother, uncle, Aunt Lana and the rest of the Caines, and start the Bowbells Arts Council; when I do, someone asks, in an interview for the county newspaper, "Poetry, what's it good for?"

I say, "Making wishes come true."

This is what I think as I sit next to Mason, the sky magenta, which is a shade of red, the clouds, wispy and white. "Trouble is not my lover . . ." I tell him.

I rock my chair:

Not my lover,

not.

Band Wives

I was a little girl when I first noticed how trouble comes when you're most certain it won't. Only recently I sent away for a pamphlet by Ann Landers which tells how all children raised by idiots feel this way. My idiot was my father who, in one minute, cried in his whiskey about how proud I made him and, in the next, hit me. So I took pleasure in church, picturing myself successful as I prayed and sang, my Heavenly Father beaming down. Once I testified to that effect and the minister said I was swell-headed, bent for hell. My mother came to my defense but always after the fact and by the time I woke up one morning in Watonga, Tennessee, I'd seen the inside of too many motel rooms, also truck cabs, the kind with berths.

What does this have to do with Galen?

I was looking for something.

I met him when he was in a band called Stoned Lonesome and driving a school bus on weekdays, going off-route to follow me as I walked the two miles from my apartment over the bakery to my job as secretary for the lumberyard. It was embarrassing, arriving for work with a yellow bus on my heels, kids screaming. Galen was embarrassing too in the outfits he'd put together from clothes he found in rag barrels. He thought he'd be delivered any day from Watonga to Nashville, inducted into the Hall of Fame finally, this white building with pictures of dead singers in it. I thought the plan was flawed.

We went out and he stayed overnight the first night and every night after.

We drank Coca-Cola for breakfast because we were always hung over. Sundays, we drove somewhere for a tour: The Sod House at Oolaweed Prairie, The Grotto of Woodcarving in Selma City, Crystal Caves. That's where we got engaged. Our tour guide had turned the overhead lights off so we could see the stalactites glow and Galen kissed me and said, loud enough for everyone to hear, "I want to be your lover always." It was from a song. I found out about his debts by accident.

"So why did he borrow money?" I asked Polly, this girl he was raised with who people around here call his cousin. She's pretty, but big. She burned her knockers once, carrying a pot of boiling potatoes.

"For a P.A.," she said. "His dad raised money for him."

"And he didn't pay it back?"

She said, "You're good for him."

Galen's dad, whose name is Tubby, was playing with a band called the Poptoppers then, and one night after we'd all eaten dinner together I was doing dishes and I asked Galen's mother, "Was there ever a time when you wished you hadn't married a musician?"

"You're running out of suds," she said.

"Galen's mother had trouble," Polly said later, when I tried on a wedding dress I'd found upstairs in the attic. "She stopped going to hear Tubby play and he had an affair."

"A long time ago?" I asked.

"Before I was born," Polly said.

I asked Galen's brother's wife, Billie Jae, "Do you go hear Eugene play just to make sure he isn't having an affair?" Eugene was playing with Galen in the Stoned Lonesome then.

She said, "I go hear Eugene play to let him know I think he's good."

I asked Galen's grandma, even though Galen's grandpa was dead. She said, "He hit me on the butt with the fiddle the night I met him."

I was having bad faith, or warnings. I couldn't tell.

We were riding back from a gig one night, a full moon shining, a hot wind blowing, and Galen beside me singing. And I realized that how I worried didn't matter. "A plan is laid," I said. Galen said, "Let's stop up here for coffee and a cheeseburger."

We got married and Galen's mother fainted from the heat.

I was thinking about the paternity suit and I missed the part where the minister says to cleave as one.

The day before the wedding, a Friday I remember, I came home from work, and the boys at the lumberyard had just given me a steam iron for a wedding present. I drove straight to Galen's folks' and his dad was asleep, his mother was in the barn. Galen was moping.

"What's wrong?" I said.

He said, "If you don't want to marry me now, don't."

Polly walked in the room with his new suit and a lint brush. "Don't be jealous," she said. "This happened before Galen met you."

He pulled on his mustache hairs then and paced the floor. And Polly said that a man from the courthouse had come by that day and served papers. "The mother was married," she said, "until the husband decided the kid didn't look like him and took a blood test."

"I never had an inkling," Galen said.

Something else was on my mind then: should I marry Galen, whose jemson wasn't always firm and he had no special knack for foreplay?

All brides have worries.

Galen left the room and Polly said, "He has a strong drive."

I said, "Galen?"

He walked back in and said, "It always seemed like a dream I was marrying a girl like you, Mae." He's a tall man and he looked sad. His neck was sunburned and I touched it, and my fingers left those white marks. "This is a money problem," I said. "That's all."

There are four bars in the Watonga area that hire bands:
The Pink Door

The Blue Moon
The Tokyo
The Hole of Foxes.
And there were more before they shut the fort down.
We were in The Hole of Foxes one night, watching the waitresses who are paid to drink and dance with the customers. I was sitting with Eugene's wife, Billie Jae, also Dynetta Blaine who is married to Tommy, the leader of Stoned Lonesome, and a fat woman who the drummer picked up. Dynetta said, "It's important to play your best every night because you never know who's in the audience."

Billie Jae said, "But you know by looking who isn't." She stood up and danced.

"Her top is cute," Dynetta said, pointing her cigarette at Billie Jae, whose top was black and fringed. Then she told me about the nice clothes she used to have when she lived in the Pontiac with Tommy and sang in Alabama, West Virginia, Ohio, once as far west as Arizona. "We made a living," she said, and she was wearing silver eye shadow, and she's pretty except for those teeth. She said, "You know the rest, how I had Frank in a motel and, but for God's grace, I would've had Karma in the car. Then we settled down."

"Good night, thank you, good night . . ."

The lights came on and Billie Jae said, "It's your turn to make eggs, Loretta Lynn."

She was talking to Dynetta.

And we were driving to Tommy and Dynetta's, and I said, "Billie Jae has a mean streak."

Galen said, "She's a whore."

I've known other girls like Billie Jae but I never figured on one for kin. She has a tattoo.

Galen said, "She's pretty if you like her kind, and Eugene does."

I had a cup of coffee and no eggs that night, and the reason I recall it is Tommy was mean too, telling Dynetta to cover her mouth when she laughed so no one would see her missing teeth. She said, "It seemed like one day one was aching and the next day both were gone."

Karma, their girl, who's seven, walked around in her pajamas and showed me a big cardboard box, the kind a refrigerator or stove comes in, and said, "I figure I could live in this if I had to."

On the way home Galen said, "We've got to get organized."

We passed The Hole of Foxes.

The Blue Moon loomed ahead, lights out, a straggly car in its lot.

I said, "I know there's a door we haven't opened yet."

The days before we were married I'd come home from work and Galen would be back from his bus route, and we'd eat sandwiches and watch soap operas and get the blanket out and get romantic on the floor, unzipping and rearranging. Most of the time he'd get soft and we'd pretend he wasn't, until he'd say, "Finish yourself up, Mae, if you have to."

And he'd run his hands softly along my legs and kiss me as I did.

Some men I'd been with who were more exciting had hurt me.

I asked myself: how many minutes in the day do you actually screw? Five? Ten? It wasn't important. But our wedding changed that.

We were supposed to stay at Galen's folks' that night and Galen said he wasn't planning on making love because someone, his dad particularly, might hear, and I started crying and we went back to town and for a joke someone had tied a cowbell to our bedsprings.

We got rid of it but too late.

After that, we made love all the way just once, in a motel, after Galen took this Jesus picture down and hid it. Otherwise he'd say I was unfeminine for trying hard, or tired. "You have to get up early," he'd say.

So when my monthlies stopped I knew I wasn't pregnant.

I felt fine.

But the doctor called it female trouble and said I needed to go to Memphis. I made an appointment and took time off work, but it rained and I'd left the car windows open. Galen found feed sacks for me to sit on and I left, waving, my butt damp, hayseeds poking through my dress. I drove around and looked at the hazy green fields, the yellow flowers, steam rising off of all of it. I stopped and bought myself an ice cream, drove some more, and came home.

"What did the special doctor say?" Galen asked.

I thought of an answer:

"To be patient," I said.

I felt something inside, growing.

We were at The Tokyo.

Dynetta, Billie Jae, me, also the fat woman Larry picked up who was getting to be a steady thing. And the band went on break, and Galen and I went outside. He put his arm around me, looked at the stars, and said, "Some special people are coming by tonight, Mae."

He'd answered an ad in the Memphis paper that said a singer and songwriter was looking for another singer to help get his show off the ground.

Galen said, "He's bringing his wife and he'll set in for a while."

Their names were James and Marie.

I knew who they were right off. James tall and good-looking in a black-checkered shirt and a white Resistol hat, Marie with long hair and one of those shiny jackets with the name of a band or dance hall on the back. They sat down and he drank beer. She had a bottle of vodka and every once in a while she'd put some in her Coke.

And the band went on break. Galen talked to them and brought them over to our table, where Tommy and Larry and Eugene were.

Galen said, "This is a buddy of mine from Laconia, I want him to sing a few."

Eugene said, "I don't remember you being in Laconia."

Billie Jae smiled at James and said, "Hush your mouth." She was talking to Eugene.

Dynetta said to Marie, "Sit here with us, honey."

So Marie sat down and took her coat off. The band went back to the stage, and James had a fine voice and his harmonies with Galen sounded silky.

I could tell Marie thought so too. And Billie Jae said, "Did you make that top?"

Marie said, nervous it seemed, "You can tell?"

You could, not because it was sloppy. The bodice was red and cream-colored calico and the long sleeves were made from sheer, lacy stuff.

It was too cute to get in a store.

Billie Jae said, "The leftover curtain pieces give it away."

Dynetta said, "It's nice to economize when you can."

Marie sipped her Coke through a straw. "Thank you," she said. She had braces on her teeth. She was pretty enough to be on TV. She leaned close to me and said, "I paid $3.79 a yard for it."

Larry's girlfriend said, "You were the Nolemretaw Queen." Nolemretaw is watermelon spelled backwards, the name of a festival in Laconia.

Marie smiled and said yes. Billie Jae said she herself was entering the Tight-Fitting Jeans Contest next time we gigged in Vinnedale.

James and Marie left then, and the rest of us ate breakfast at our place above the bakery. Galen started right off talking about how James could play six instruments and he'd written a lot of songs.

Tommy said, "Four men's plenty. We don't get paid enough as it is."

Dynetta shuddered.

Galen said, "But if he joined us we'd play in pricey clubs in towns like Little Rock, Jackson, Birmingham."

"Nashville," Billie Jae said.

"No," Eugene said.

Galen said, "Someday."

Tommy said, "I'm not leaving, and you're not either."

They went home.

Galen and I went out our back door and stood on the roof and looked at Watonga—it shuts down hard.

"I wonder what lies ahead," Galen said.

I didn't answer. I was pressing on my belly. It didn't hurt.

A week later, the night of a gig at The Blue Moon, James and Marie came by our house first, and James said, "That old guy is a has-been and everybody else is a never-will-be." Galen and I were sitting at the table eating, and James stood there, hat in his hand.

Marie paced around and looked at my knickknacks.

Galen said, "But it's Tommy's P.A."

James said, "We'll borrow money and get a new one."

I said, "What happened to your P.A., Galen, the one your dad bought?"

He picked the pineapple off his Chicken Waikiki and shook his head.

James said, "They'll hold us back."

Marie said, "I'll make matching shirts, pale blue, I think."

I envisioned it.

Galen, since I'd trimmed his hair and got him clothes, was handsome, masculine in the body and delicate in the face: red lips, black eyelashes, cheekbones high and pointy. "This song is dedicated to my wife, Mae," he'd say, and famous people would be watching.

The TV camera would flash to me.

We went to The Blue Moon that night, and Tommy plunked bad notes on purpose. James sang about lovers who had a bond of the heart and one day it broke as one of them stayed out late and the other turned in early. "We never believed our Silver Rhythm would ever leave," he sang. Galen did sliding bottleneck chords and shook his hips.

James and Galen announced afterwards, with James doing the talking, that they were going off together and the last gig for Stoned Lonesome was next week. Galen pulled his mustache hairs, and Billie Jae grabbed his belt and said he was betraying Eugene. It was her turn to cook eggs and come over to eat and talk it over please.

Tommy said, "I'm not hungry. If you think you're getting your P.A. back, Galen, you're crazy."

Larry sat there. He goes where Tommy goes because they've been together years. Dynetta said, "We had our chance. Now let these young people have theirs." She said, "Don't be a stranger, Mae."

So the rest of us ate breakfast (James, Marie, Billie Jae, Eugene, Galen, me) and Billie Jae talked how Eugene plays bass and rhythm guitar and sings if he doesn't have to harmonize. James nodded and drank coffee and said his plans for the future included scouting out Memphis, and if he didn't like it he was going to Nashville.

I shivered, thinking of Dynetta saying good musicians are a dime a dozen there, sleeping in gutters. Billie Jae said, "Let me help. I used to work in Memphis." Marie and I were washing dishes and Marie said, loud enough for just me to hear, "I bet she did."

Billie Jae heard it. "Well, Galen did too," she said.

"When," I said.

She said, "His wild days."

It was settled then that James and Galen were going to Memphis in the morning and Eugene and Billie Jae were riding along. Driving home, I asked Galen, first, why he let Tommy have his P.A., second, did he owe money, and, third, when did he live in Memphis and how wild was he? A husband and wife shouldn't have secrets.

He said, "The difference between a man and woman, Mae, is more than how they pee." He pushed the gas pedal down and the car swaggered.

In bed, I tried to hold his face and talk sense and he did a strange thing: slid my hand to his jemson, which was hard as ice. I lay still, one hand on the cold jemson, the other on my hot belly, and thought how my father had foretold bad weather with his leg.

The day they left, Marie came to stay overnight with me, and she made pizza and set my hair. We drank vodka and she opened her mouth to show me her braces, a rubber band stretching from one side to the other. "I can't wait to get them off," she said. And in the middle of the night, she rolled over, hugged me, rubbed my stomach, and said, "I love you, honey." She was thinking of James. He called the next day to say Memphis was a bust and he was set on Nashville now. Billie Jae was a fool and no way was Eugene in his band.

Marie hung up. "That can't be the whole story," she said.

Then Galen came home and told me James and Eugene had wanted to go to a bar with strippers, and Billie Jae wouldn't let Eugene. When James went, she followed him in there, yanked on his clothes, slapped him, threw beer in his face, yelled, and got thrown out.

"Why did she care if James went?" I said.

Galen shrugged.

"Where were you?"

"Shopping," he said.

He gave me two presents, a DustBuster vacuum cleaner and a blue dress.

The last gig was at The Pink Door. Galen went early and I was supposed to come by later with his dinner. I opened a can of tuna and Polly, who was sitting at my kitchen table, said, "He hates tuna."

That's not true but he'd had a sandwich for lunch and no vegetable. So I heated a casserole and put the lid on and put it in a bag.

We sat down with Dynetta and Marie, and Larry's fat girlfriend.

"If they could draw a last-night crowd like this all the time they wouldn't have to split up," Polly said.

"Where's Billie Jae?" I asked everybody.

"She's coming later," Dynetta said.

And the band went on break, and I gave Galen the bag. He looked inside it and said, "Let's go for a walk." We sat in the car in the parking lot. "Don't ever bring me a casserole in the bar again," he said. He was thinking of Nashville, I suppose, eating a casserole in a high-tone bar while a talent scout watched. He took the fork out of the bag. "Real good, though," he said, chewing.

We went back inside and Billie Jae was there. She stuck her butt in my face and said, "It was rigged. I didn't even make the finalists." She was talking about the Tight-Fitting Jeans Contest. She'd driven to Vinnedale and entered it. "I figure we'd never play there again," she said, "because Eugene's going to play with Tubby and the Poptoppers now and work the farm with his mom."

She was drinking hard, walking around talking to people, pointing at me and Marie.

"She stands behind Eugene," Polly said.

James started singing and people clapped, and Billie Jae pointed, waved her fists, and yelled, "He's the problem. He's the problem."

Marie said, "I'll kill her."

She crossed the room and dragged Billie Jae outside by the arm.

Billie Jae was yelling: "She's hurting me. Ouch, ouch, ouch."

"Why do people find her attractive?" Polly said.

I said, "Billie Jae?"

Polly shook her head. "No, Marie."

Then they came inside and sat down, and Billie Jae cried.

Marie said, "I slapped some sense into her. Now one of us should walk down to the Quik Trip and get her black coffee and aspirin."

Larry's girlfriend leaned across the table, and said, "Honey, when you can't see through to the next phase, life's changing for the best."

Billie Jae blew her nose.

I put my coat on and went to the Quik Trip.

As I waited for change, I read the magazines: EDDIE FISHER FELL FOR LIZ ON MERCY MISSION, CAMPSITE OF MUMMIES FOUND IN UTAH DESERT.

It was like a balloon inside, letting go.

I'd always pictured the clinic in Memphis, how it would look, white walls and chrome, a bald man standing over me, smiling, saying, "Tell me where it hurts, dear." It didn't. The doctor explained that: "The body accommodates slow growth." She was a woman, and it was the Laconia hospital, not Memphis. Marie drove me there.

But first I went back to the bar, and the band was on break. I couldn't find Billie Jae. She was with Galen in our car. He was sitting there, his shirt unbuttoned halfway from the bottom up, and he was holding the tails out of the way. Her head was going up and down. Eugene came up behind me and said, "I'm not sure they ever quit, but it's been a while since they've been caught."

It wasn't pain exactly.

Galen leaned over me, his clothes disheveled, and said, "I wanted to be good enough but I'm not." In the car, on the way to the hospital, Marie said: "If James did that to me I'd glue his hand to his dick."

They opened me up and found out the cyst had burst, and closed me again.

I was laying in bed for the second day in a row, and Galen's dad walked in with a teapot with mums in it. He set it by my bed. "Galen's ma sent these," he said. "She'd be here herself but she's upset and locked in the barn, and won't come out." He gave me a prayer book Galen's grandma sent with categories for special occasions:

On a Birthday

Of a Wife

For Precious Fruits

Over the Bed of Sickness.

"Thank you," I said. He took his hat off and said, "I knew Galen was pussy-simple but I always figured if he settled down he'd get over it and wouldn't go around all the time like a year-old stud."

Polly visited me. "You were blind with love," she said.

Marie called me eleven months later and I went to The Hole of Foxes to see her. It was redecorated, the walls painted black and Christmas tree lights and icicles hanging down. James had his new band. Marie said, "I didn't want to take Galen and Billie Jae to Nashville with us, but James insisted. Galen kept coming to important gigs drunk and Billie Jae picked fights. And we ditched them."

"You got your braces off," I said.

She said, "Is your bedroom door swinging yet?"

I told her about Dale, whose wife lost sixty-nine pounds on Weight Watchers and started sleeping around on him, and they got a divorce and now we go out. "Three or four nights a week," I said. "I met him at the lumberyard." I leaned close. "What happened to your tooth?"

One of the big front ones was gray.

"It was always like that," she said. "My braces just hid it."

I said, "Do you need money to fix it?"

She said, "No. Did I tell you that Billie Jae had a baby?"

I thought of my scar, four inches long and crisscrossed like railroad tracks. James was singing loud, and I remembered the night I'd reached across the bed and touched Galen's jemson, which was lovely because I couldn't have it. "I want Silver Rhythm," I'd said. He answered: "You act like a whore, Mae." Now Dale gets hard as soon as I'm near and follows me around with his quivering like a divining stick. "I'm going to marry Dale," I said, "and you can tell Galen that." It was the first time I'd thought of it. He hadn't asked me yet. And the new guitar player did a sliding bottleneck chord, and James sang, "We never believed, oh we never believed our Silver Rhythm would ever leave."

What was it? How do you know you have it? What was Marie's future?

These were my questions.

"Do you like your job? How's your boyfriend? What're your plans? How's life, Mae?" It was Marie talking. I looked at her. Tinsel revolved on the ceiling fan above us. She smiled. That bad tooth was still bothering me.